A&B  Publications & Productions

# Adam's Prep

Volume 1

New Jersey: A&B Publications and Productions

All characters represented in this book are fictional.

Cover designed by Aly Hunt Smith.

Dedicated to my two little boys who mean everything to me. Special thanks to Ben, my family, Irene and Janel for all your help and encouragement.

## Chapter 1

The screen door slammed, as I headed down the back steps and through the yard. I knew if Dad was home he'd yell at me to watch the door, or I'd break it. I wasn't sure why exactly I was rushing, I just needed to get to the lake, and have some time there before I went out. High school was starting in exactly two days, and I was a nervous wreck. Change scared me a lot, and this was definitely a big change. I knew that a few quiet hours next to the water, with the sun shining down on me, was just about the only thing that could calm me down.

I lifted the rusty handle on the old, iron gate in the back corner of the yard. The blueberry bushes that ran along it didn't have a single berry left on them. It was hard to believe that only about a month ago they had been so full of the sweet, juicy little berries. Summer always went by so fast. I was only fourteen years old and already it seemed like everything good in life went by too quickly. This past year eighth grade had flown by, and now I was leaving my small, comfortable elementary school and starting at a new, giant high school in two days.

But for this afternoon at least, I could still pretend that it was summer. It may have been the day after Labor Day, but it was still hot and sunny. I could lie in the sun at my favorite spot by the lake and pretend it wasn't all about to happen. I walked the short distance through the field in the back of our yard, and came to the edge of the lake. I loved this place. It was quiet and beautiful. The grass went right up to the sandy beach, where eventually the sand turned into a million little pebbles that lined the bottom of the lake. Tall pine trees bordered the edge of the water, and the sun poked through their branches to shine down and reflect on the brown surface in tiny, golden pools.

Only in South Jersey could I be a half an hour from the beach, a half an hour from Philadelphia, and live on an old peach farm, with a private little lake in back of my house. I loved my house. It had been my Gram's house before, and my Great Gram's before that. It was a huge, old, white farm house with green shutters. It wasn't a peach farm anymore, and most of the land had been sold, but there were still a few peach trees on the side of the house, the blueberry bushes, and Great-Gram's rosebushes. My dad had renovated a lot of the inside to make it new and modern looking, but the outside looked exactly like it did a hundred years ago.

When we learned about New Jersey history in seventh grade, I used to like to think a lot about what life must have been like around here a hundred years ago. Who were the people who had built this house and first lived in it? What were their lives like? Who did they love? What were their secrets? For some reason I always pictured life as being much simpler then. I bet they didn't have to go to a big, strange high school with tons of kids they'd never seen before. I bet they just got to live on their farm, take buggy rides to the beach, bake peach pies, and sit by the same lake I was staring at right now. I bet it was OK to be quiet back then, too. I hate how people always ask me why I'm so quiet. It's not that I'm really that quiet; I just think a lot, and I don't think I'm quite ready yet to say all the things that come to mind.

Today though, I really didn't want to think at all. I wished all my worries would go away, so I could just lay by the lake and relax. I spread out my old quilt, lay down against the soft, worn cotton and closed my eyes. The sun began to warm my body. That is simply the best feeling in the world. Sometimes I think the warm glow of the sun on my face, arms, and legs could wash away any problem I might have.

I felt the ground hard beneath me, and I could smell the familiar scent of the cedar water. Some people, like my sister Kelly, think cedar water is gross. It has sort of a funny smell, and a murky, brownish color, but I think the lake is absolutely beautiful. My sister, my Dad and I, our little McKinney family, had lived in this house for almost nine years now and I loved everything about it.

I was thinking again, I couldn't help it. It's an addicting habit, yes, I know. It always seems like I'm incapable of clearing my mind. My thoughts started tumbling through my head as they always do. I thought about how our house was just one of the many differences between Kelly and me. Kelly is my twin sister, my complete opposite, and, *usually*, my best friend.

I could spend every afternoon sitting here at the lake doing nothing at all. Kelly, on the other hand, is restless here. She always needs to go somewhere, or do something. Most afternoons Kelly prefers to be at the mall, or at a friend's house, and the few days she spends at home, she never ventures outside. She mainly plays on the internet, shopping, chatting on AIM, or updating her status on Facebook. Kelly has over 400 Facebook friends. I have about 70. Believe me this is only the start of our differences. We may be twins, but besides our looks, we are very, very different.

Even our looks aren't that much alike. We're fraternal twins, not identical; we look just like any regular siblings might. We're both blondes, and we both have green eyes that people usually assume are blue because they don't take the time to really look. But for some reason this assumption only bothers me, she could care less. Kelly is two inches taller, and thinner than I am. She's been dancing since we were two, and she has the body of a dancer. I quit dancing sometime around Kindergarten because I hated the recitals. The crowds, the spotlight, the nervousness – it just wasn't for me. Also, I don't have Kelly's dancer build. I'm a little thicker, but I'm not heavy. I'd kill for her long, muscular legs though. She keeps her blonde hair long, so she can put it in a bun for dance, or a high pony tail for cheerleading. My hair is cut in a short bob that frames my face. I keep it that way, so that I can hide behind the strands of it when I start to feel nervous.

We dress pretty differently, too. Kelly loves *Hollister*, and it fits her perfectly. With her cute build and long blonde hair, she could model as the typical Jersey shore "surfer girl". Kelly looks great in jean shorts, a bright tank top, and flip flops. She's basically been wearing that exact outfit all summer.

My taste is a little different. I like to wear clothes that make me look older and more mature than I am. I know everyone thinks I'm one of those smart kids who acts way too old for her age, but I'm not really, I just feel more comfortable in plainer clothes. If an outfit is going to draw attention to me, I usually steer away from it. I like wearing khaki shorts and a polo shirt, crisp white capris with a navy shirt, or a sweater and jeans in winter. This summer I've taken to wearing sundresses: flowered, plain, short, long – all different types. I found a picture of my mom, and she was wearing the most beautiful, light blue, flowered sundress. She looked so pretty that I figured even though I can't really see too much of a resemblance between us, if they looked good on her, I could try and pull it off too.

The differences between Kelly and me don't end at our appearances. We couldn't possibly have more opposite personalities and interests. Kelly is a people person and I, definitely, am not. She loves the spotlight. I love a good book. Whether she's dancing on stage, cheering at a game, or hanging out with our friends, Kelly loves to be the center of attention. For the most part I don't mind, she's great at it. There are times though, when having a twin sister that's great at everything can get a little old.

Kelly can make anyone smile, just by smiling at them. Her grin could light up an entire room, which is a good thing, because she uses it often. I don't know how, but Kelly is always happy. She's always on the go, with a new plan or idea. When we grow up, she wants to move to New York City and go to all the big clubs, and fancy parties, and meet famous people. She plans on being a dancer on Broadway. Ludicrous, right? Well, if there's someone who will actually make a dream like that happen, then it's Kelly. Of course millions of girls dream about a career as a professional dancer, but my sister will be the one to really do it. That's just the way she is. She never lets anything get in the way of her goals, and it seems like everybody she meets along the way loves her.

As I said, I'm nothing like Kelly. The spotlight terrifies me. Last year at Eighth Grade Graduation I had to give a speech because I was the Valedictorian, and I literally almost passed out. It wasn't that I wasn't happy to get the award, I had worked really hard to earn it and grades are super important to me, it was just the speech. I hate getting up in front of a crowd. I like to focus on the quiet things in life: movie nights with my best friends, good books, lying by the lake, the beach, and getting good grades. As my Dad always puts it, Kelly is a talker and I'm a thinker. They both have their up and downs.

There is one other thing that's very different about Kelly and me – Jake Williams. Yep, believe it or not, I have a boyfriend and Kelly has never had one. We're pretty serious too. We've been dating since September of eighth grade and we plan on staying together in high school since we're both going to Adam's Prep. It may seem surprising that I'm the one who has a boyfriend, but if you think about it, it's not. I'm comfortable and I don't have to be shy because I know Jake so well. I can be myself around him, just like I can with my best friends. We spend a lot of time doing quiet things, just the two of us, and I never have to feel nervous in a crowd or around other people because I know he's always there. Plus I know I can trust Jake. I know I'm probably too young to say this, but I love him, and he loves me. Jake is kind of like having that soft, comfy teddy that you carried around as a kid whenever you were scared and he made everything better, except Jake also comes with gorgeous blue eyes, a nice body, and a great smile. Yep, Jake forced Teddy B. right into retirement.

While I absolutely love going out with Jake, Kelly claims she'll never have a boyfriend until she's thirty. She thinks it will tie her down too much. She talks to about three different boys a night on her cell, and I can't even imagine how many on the computer. She loves to meet new people, go new places, and she can't wait to start high school tomorrow. I, however, have never been so nervous in my life. At least I'll have her with me though, and that does make it a little better. It's weird, we may be total opposites, but I still really need her. I think in the end, it comes down to the fact that we complement each other well. If we were too much alike, we might get jealous of each other, or not get along. Of course that still happens sometimes, but most of the time, she's my best friend.

My daydreaming was interrupted when I heard Jake's brother's truck pulling up onto the gravel, before I heard him call my name.

"Katie?" he yelled, "You down there?"

"Yeah," I replied. "Come on down."

I heard Jake tell his brother, Trey, to pick him up in two hours, so that he could go to football practice, and then he came sprinting across the field towards the lake. As he got closer, he slowed down a little, and a slight look of nervousness came over his face, like it did every time he realized we would be alone. His cheeks started to blush a little, as his mouth turned up into a shy smile. It was so cute how after a year, I could still make him a little nervous.

"How are you?" he asked with an adorable smile.

"I'm OK, I'm dreading starting school!"

"Kates! It's gonna be fun!" he said, as he sat down on the blanket.

"I'll probably get lost. The building is so big, and we've never switched classes before. I know I'll be that dorky freshman wandering the halls and trying to look at the map they gave us in our orientation packets!" I said, in only a half-joking manner.

Jake laughed, "You will not. If you could figure out those Algebra problems you used to ace last year in Math, I'm sure you can figure out the layout of Adam's Prep."

"That's not the point!" I said in frustration. "At St. Anne's we all just stayed in one nice, comfy room, with one teacher, and I knew everybody. At Adam's Prep I barely know anyone."

"Kate, it won't be so bad!" Jake replied. He relaxed a little and lay down on the blanket next to me. "It's not like you don't know anybody. All of your best friends are going there; Kelly is going there; most of our eighth grade class is going there; and most importantly, I'm going there. We'll still be together." As he said this, Jake's hand found mine on the blanket, and wrapped around it. His touch was warm and soft. We had been dating almost a year, but it still sent tingles down my spine.

"I know," I whispered, not joking around at all anymore, "but it's so big, and there are so many kids I don't know yet."

I debated whether to tell Jake the truth: that new things and new people make me really nervous. So nervous in fact, that I couldn't sleep at all last night. Sometimes I felt comfortable enough to tell Jake my real feelings. Other times there were still things about me that I kept hidden. I didn't think Jake could ever really understand my shyness, or how much it affected me every day. Jake was like Kelly, being around people and making friends came easily to him. In some ways it was awesome, he always looked out for me, he made me feel safe when I was nervous, and he helped me to be less shy. Other times I felt like no matter how close we became, he would never really know the real me. I was worried that if I told him, he'd think I was weird.

"Earth to Katie," Jake said as he tickled my side. "Katie, are you in there?"

"Sorry! I was just thinking about school………and you," I admitted.

"Well, in that case, think away! I must be awfully nice to think about," Jake teased.

"Who said I was thinking good things about you?" I joked back. "Maybe I was thinking about how I need a new boyfriend."

"Oh yeah?" He replied as a smile spread under his big, blue eyes. "I bet I can change your mind." Jake sat up a little on his elbow and leaned over me. His face blocked the sun and I could look up clearly at him. His blonde hair fell forward on his face as he closed his eyes and leaned in towards me. I closed my eyes and felt his lips begin to touch mine, and I could smell his scent. After a full year of being his girlfriend, he had become so incredibly exciting and comforting at the same time. As he kissed me, I blocked out everything except thoughts of him.

The kiss was soft, slow and amazing.

"Ok," I said, "I guess I'll keep you around for awhile."

"That's a good thing, because I had absolutely no intention of letting you go," he replied. He wrapped his arms around me, and I lay my head on his shoulder. I wanted the moment to never end.

After what felt like minutes, but must have been hours, we heard the unmistakable sound of Trey's truck coming up the gravel driveway.

"I have to get to practice," Jake said. "Have fun with your friends tonight, and I'll call you tomorrow." He squeezed my hand.

"OK," I said, and suddenly I realized that this was the last moment that we'd see each other before high school began. After this everything would be different. I leaned over and gave him a hug goodbye. In my head I tried to remember all the details of our afternoon: the kiss, his smile, the hot sun on our faces. Maybe if I could remember it all perfectly I could freeze time right here and never really have to move on.

## Chapter 2

I stood and watched Trey's truck pull off down the road, then leaned down, rolled up my blanket and headed back to the house. I stopped in the kitchen, grabbed a Coke and went up to my room to check my email. There was one thing I was looking forward to today – all of my best friends were having one last sleepover before school began. Even though I was nervous about school starting, I couldn't wait for our sleepover. They're always so much fun.

I plopped down on my bed, and looked around my room as I waited for my laptop to start up. Kelly and I had redecorated our rooms two years ago. They were the last projects that Dad did in our house, and we got to pick out exactly how we wanted them. My room is light blue and white. I picked those colors because they remind me of the beach, which besides the lake, is my favorite place to be. Three of my walls are all blue, and one is blue and white striped. I have sheer, white curtains, and a matching blue and white striped comforter. Dad built bookcases into the wall to hold all my books. I love to read and I read them all over and over, so I save every single one. There has to be over 200 books already lined up on the shelves. My furniture is white, and my dresser is covered in pictures that are all in different, pretty frames. There are pictures of Kelly and me; my eighth grade class picture; pictures of me with my best friends Kelly, Gopi, Jada, and Gia; pictures of Grammy; pictures of Dad, Kelly and me; and then one single picture in an old silver frame of my mom.

I set my laptop down and walked over to pick it up. It was a picture of her holding Kelly and me in her lap on our first birthday. There was a giant, pink, princess cake in front of us, and party hats on all of our heads. I ran my finger gently over my mom's face in the picture and tried for the millionth time to identify all the parts of me that looked like her.

"What are you doing, Kate?"

I jumped a little and quickly set the picture down, as Kelly walked over.

"Kate, you're not looking at that again are you? It always just makes you sad," Kelly said in a gentle tone.

"I can't help it. I think about her, Kell. I think about her all the time. She's out there, and we have no idea where. Some town, somewhere, in some house our mom lives every day. Don't you ever wonder where she is? Who she's with? What she's doing? What she looks like?" Familiar tears started to well up behind my eyes, and I bit my lip to hold them back.

When I looked up at Kelly there were no tears behind her eyes, only anger, as usual. Her gentleness had quickly turned to frustration when I had tried to talk to her about our mom. Anytime I tried to talk about Mom, Kelly got angry. She had never forgiven her.

"No, I don't think about her, because I'm pretty sure she never thinks about us. And I may not know where she lives, but I know exactly who she's with: the man she left us for. That guy who was so important to her that she walked out on Dad, her family, and us," Kelly walked over to the window, still holding the picture and staring out as she talked.

"We were three, Kate. She left us when we were three years old. It takes a real special kind of asshole to walk out on their two little girls and never look back." Kelly turned her head from the picture in disgust.

She was right. I knew Mom had left us, her family, to run off with another guy. I knew she had never called. I knew the only contact we'd had from her was a random Christmas card that first year, and then a card on our tenth birthday that she sent to Grandma Smith's house, because she didn't even know where we lived. I knew that all those soccer games, birthdays, holidays, graduations, and awards she had missed, had all been her fault, and I knew that every one of the hundreds of nights that I had cried myself to sleep because I missed her, had all been her fault. I knew it, and yet, I still missed her. I hadn't forgiven her either, but I also didn't know how to forget about her like Kelly had.

Kelly had moved on. Dad had moved on. They had taken down every single picture of her, thrown out all of her stuff, got rid of her Christmas stocking, her favorite coffee mug, her clothes. They had forgotten about her and made their own lives, but I still missed her. I still kept her pictures. I still slept with the tattered birthday card under my pillow. I still desperately wanted, just once, to feel her hug me. I wanted to know if she ever thought about me, because I always thought about her.

Kelly broke me out of my thoughts.

"Kate," she said, gently taking the pictures out of my hand, "don't do this. Not tonight. We are about to start high school, and we're about to have an awesome sleepover with our best friends. You need to have fun tonight; we'll never have this time again. Let her go, Katie."

My twin sister smiled at me. She genuinely didn't want me to get upset. I knew she was right, tonight was going to be fun, and I needed to enjoy myself. I smiled back, turned away from the picture, and gave Kelly a hug. Right now I needed to let my sadness go, act like any other fourteen year old girl, and enjoy my last night of summer with my friends.

....I also knew that deep down, I would never, ever be able to let my mom go.

### Chapter 3

"Ready to head out girls?" Dad said as he scraped his dish into the garbage and loaded it into the dishwasher.

"Yes!" we cried in unison.

I was so excited for our sleepover tonight, all of my best friends together one last time before we started at Adam's Prep. Kelly and I ran upstairs, grabbed our sleeping bags and the rest of our stuff, and headed out to the car to meet Dad.

"So ladies, what exactly do you have planned for tonight?" Dad teased. "I hope it includes behaving."

"What exactly do *you* have planned for tonight?" Kelly teased right back. "Is Miss Linda coming over to watch a little TV tonight?" We both broke out laughing. Dad had been casually dating a girl named Linda for about two years now. If you could even call it "*dating*" because sometimes I wondered how he ever managed to get married and have kids, when it seemed like he was absolutely clueless around women. In all honesty though, I was kind of relieved that he never seriously dated. I liked Miss Linda and all, but I wasn't exactly sure how I would handle it if he were ever in a real relationship.

"Hahaha, girls," Dad pretended to laugh, "Actually I'll be enjoying my free night by playing poker with Uncle Steve. Anyway, we're here. Have fun, be good, and I have my cell phone. Call me if you need anything at all."

I reached over the seat, wrapped my arms around his neck and leaned my cheek against his scruffy face. Even though I was fourteen years old, the way his cheeks felt against mine and the familiar scent of his cologne still comforted me.

"I love you, Dad," I whispered into his ear.

"Love you too, Kates," he said, as he ruffled my hair.

"Bye, Dad!" Kelly yelled as she jumped out of the car and raced up Gopi's driveway.

"Bye, sweet pea!" He yelled out.

I followed Kelly up the driveway and onto the Patel's porch just as she was ringing the bell. We always have our sleepovers at Gopi's house because she isn't allowed to stay over at any of our houses. The Patels are Pakistani Muslims and they follow the beliefs of their religion, which can be pretty strict at times. Gopi isn't allowed to do a lot of things that other kids are. At the same time though, Gopi understands why these rules are important to her faith. Sometimes it's hard on Gopi to balance the stress of friends and school, with family and religion. She tries to respect the beliefs of her parents, but she also really wants to be a typical, American kid. Overall though, she's done an amazing job of finding a balance between the two, and she's one of the sweetest, kindest, smartest girls that I know.

Our sleepovers are the perfect example of the balance Gopi has had to find. In the Patel household, sleeping over at another family's house is absolutely out of the question, because Gopi could be exposed to boys, drinking, or something even worse. However, Gopi has managed to convince her parents that if all of us sleepover at her house they can keep an eye on everything that's going on and she can still be a part of everything and not feel left out. We think it's a perfect compromise. We couldn't care less where our sleepovers are held, and this way Gopi always gets to be a part of them. I think Dr. Patel has wised up a little though. After the first two or three late night giggle fests, he started scheduling his night shifts on the same days that he would have five teenage girls sleeping under his roof.

"Hello, ladies," said Gopi's dad, "I never can remember who is who!"

"Dr. Patel!" Kelly exclaimed, "We're not even identical!"

"I know, I know," he replied with a sigh, "you look alike to me though. Have you eaten? Do you want some karahi? Mrs. Patel has some left over from dinner."

The Patels always offer us food when we come to their house. Gopi says its part of their culture; women are proud of the foods they cook. Gia's Nonna is Italian, and she always does the same thing if we go to her house. Both of them are amazing chefs. Home cooked food is sort of a rarity in our house. Dad tries, but dinner is never exactly gourmet. We eat a lot of frozen food from Trader Joe's, so the offer was pretty tempting. I love karahi. It's a delicious chicken dish, smothered in a spicy tomato sauce, but tonight my anxiousness to see my friends overcame my taste buds.

"No thanks, Dr. Patel, I think we'll just head up to Gopi's room if that's OK?" I asked.

"Sure. Go head up. Have fun tonight. I'll be leaving for work in a bit."

Kelly and I quickly went up the stairs and into Gopi's room. My three best friends in the world were already there, and I smiled as they jumped up to hug Kelly and I.

"What took you guys so long?" Jada exclaimed. "This is our last night before high school for the five of us to be together. We need to make this a night to remember!" I looked around at all of them as they squealed in agreement.

First there was Jada Brown. In a word, Jada is beautiful. She is half white and half black, and she has dark, curly hair, soft brown skin, and big, gorgeous, green eyes. Jada is definitely the most outgoing of our group.

She and Kelly can walk into any situation and instantly

make friends. Jada is also the most athletic. She plays

soccer, basketball and softball and she's good at all of

them. Last year in eighth grade she was named "Athlete

of the Year", and she was the Snowball Queen.  Girls,

boys, teachers, parents, coaches – everybody – love

Jada. But you know what? It never gets to her head. Jada

is one of the most unsuperficial, down-to-earth girls I've

ever met. Yeah, she's charismatic, but she uses it to make

her friends, classmates and teammates happy. Anytime

that I'm around Jada, I'm guaranteed to be smiling and

having fun. Oh yeah, and Jada is one of the only people I

know who has more Facebook friends than Kelly; I

secretly kind of like that, although I wouldn't admit that to

Kell in a million years.

Next there is Gia DeMarco. Gia is much, much quieter than Jada. She doesn't play any sports, and she isn't really into school that much either, but she loves art and has an amazing sense of style. Gia is one of the best dressers I have ever met. In fact she won the eighth grade awards for "Best Dressed" and "Best Hair". Winning both was a new school record, but Gia definitely deserved it. I think her shyness stems from her family sometimes. She's an only child, and her parents had her when they were really young, just out of high school. It's obvious that they're only still together for Gia's sake, and she knows it. I think that hurts her a lot, and I know their fighting is rough on her. She has an amazing grandmom though, her Nonna, and she spends a lot of time with her, and working on her paintings.

Finally, we have our Gopi Patel. Gopi is a tiny, dark haired, dark eyed, dark skinned Pakistani girl. One time in fourth grade I saw a movie about a beautiful little brown haired, brown eyed fairy and ever since then, that's what I've thought Gopi looked like. Once or twice I've seen her fully dressed in her traditional Middle Eastern clothes, with henna tattoos on her hands and feet, her long silk robes, and jewels in her nose and on her forehead. It was probably the most beautiful thing I've ever seen. Gopi's culture fascinates me. Their foods, their clothes, their beliefs: they're so different from mine. I think they're exotic. To Gopi though, I think they're a bit stifling. Gopi's life is pretty much defined by her faith, her culture and her family. Being a Pakistani Muslim girl in America is not easy. Gopi's parents have much stricter rules than any of ours. She is not allowed to date or talk on the phone with boys. She can't go to dances or parties where there will be boys, and she always has to dress conservatively. Gopi has explained to us that this is because her family believes that a girl should be completely innocent and pure when she meets her husband, and that her parents will actually help Gopi pick out who her husband will be. I can't even think about marriage right now, but I understand and respect Gopi's family's beliefs and traditions. It's not always so easy for her though, she is constantly trying to find a balance between her American self, and her Muslim self.

Gopi also has to balance one other thing: academics. She and I are the two bookworms of our friends. We both devote ourselves to getting straight A's and being at the top of the class. That's actually how Gopi became friends with us. When she first came to our school, she barely talked and didn't have many friends. By about fifth grade, I realized that she was a good study buddy and during our study sessions I realized that she was pretty cool to hang out with too. I started inviting her to eat lunch with us, and soon the other girls realized how great she was. Just like that, she was one of the crew.

That's pretty much it. The five of us make up an amazing group of friends and I really don't know what I would do without them. Having them in my life has made not having a mom  a lot easier, hopefully they can help make high school a lot easier too. I'm really thankful that we're all still going to be together in high school. A couple months ago, we weren't even sure that was going to happen. We all went to St. Anne's Elementary School together, but until last May, it wasn't definite that we would all be going to Adam's Prep together. Gopi had always known she would go there. Adam's is the best private, prep school in the area, and her parents really want her to get into an Ivy League college. Plus her older sister, Abhaya, went to Adam's. Jada's parents decided last winter that she would definitely go there, because they like

Adam's basketball program the best, and basketball is Jada's main sport. Gia, Kelly and I were undecided for awhile. Adam's Prep isn't cheap, and the money wasn't going to be easy on our Dad, or her parents. Luckily though, I ended up getting a scholarship, which made it much easier for Dad to afford, and at the last minute, Gia's Nonna announced she would pay for Gia's tuition as a graduation gift. So that decided it, we would all get to stay together for high school.

I looked around at all their faces and smiled.

Jada smiled back and lit up the room with her laugh, "Are you getting sentimental on us again, Katie? After Eighth Grade Graduation I'd know that look on your face anywhere!"

"We can be sentimental tonight, guys," Gia replied, "This is it, our last night before high school. We have to make the most of it. Things might never be the same again."

"Seriously," Gopi agreed, "you guys are the best friends I've ever had. This summer's been awesome. I'll never forget you guys."

"Forget us!" Kelly exclaimed. "Why in the world would you have to forget us? We're all going to Adam's Prep. We're still going to be best friends!"

"Kell, we say that," I started, "but what if things change? I don't want to lose you guys. I'm really nervous."

Jada put her arm around me. "You're not gonna lose anyone. None of us are. Let's make a pact right now that we will stay best friends in high school no matter what happens."

"Should we sign it in blood?" Gia asked.

"Ew, Gi, you're so dramatic!" Jada replied. "No. Let's all just put our hands in and make a pact to be friends forever. Nothing can come between us."

So we did. Kelly, Jada, Gopi, Gia and I all put our hands in the middle and grabbed onto each other's hands. Mine and Kelly's hands looked similar, Gopi's were tiny, Gia had black nails, and Jada had bright pink, but somehow they all fit. They looked like they belonged together. For the first time in a long time I felt like everything was going to be OK. I fit somewhere. I belonged with these girls. Somehow with them by my side, high school didn't seem quite so bad anymore.

## Chapter 4

I had never in my life had to ride on a bus before. To make matters worse, it was coming at 6:30 am every day to pick up Kelly and me. Then we would have to sit on it for an hour while it picked up all the kids going to Hammonton High School, the public school in my town, dropped them off, and then drove to Adam's Prep.

Kelly and I stood on the corner in our matching Adam's uniforms. She, of course, had rolled her skirt up a few times and accessorized perfectly with makeup and jewelry. I tried rolling my skirt, but I thought my thighs looked too big, and I had only put on a little mascara and lip gloss. Somehow Kelly had managed to look adorable on our first day, and I felt completely blah.

Slowly, the big, yellow monstrosity of a bus pulled up to the corner. I had never been a kid who was too concerned with being popular, but I had a strange feeling that if I did want to have even the tiniest bit of popularity in high school, showing up on a bus every day was definitely not a step in the right direction. We climbed up the steps, and Kelly smiled, and said hi to the bus driver who, in return, grumbled at her to find a seat.

As Kelly looked around at the unfamiliar faces, trying to determine where to sit, my first waves of panic started to come. My stomach felt sick, my face flushed, and I stared at the floor so I wouldn't have to make eye contact with anyone. Once she started walking, I followed Kelly back to the seat she picked.

"This is horrible!" I whispered to her.

"Kate, it's not that bad. We'll get used to it; we just have to learn to wake up a little earlier."

"It's not waking up I care about. It's all these strange kids. I feel like everyone's looking at us," I said in the lowest voice possible.

"They probably are," Kelly said with a little annoyance in her voice. "We're the new kids. Everybody always checks out who the new kids are. Plus we're wearing these silly uniforms. You would stare at us too. No one's being mean or anything; chill out, Kate. You already hate school and you haven't even given it a chance."

I decided not to reply because Kelly's response really annoyed me. In fact at that moment, I didn't just hate school, I also hated Kelly. I hated her for always being so laid back. I hated her because meeting people didn't scare her. I hated her because she saw starting high school as fun and exciting, and here I was just trying to make it through the first day without either passing out, or throwing up from nervousness.

I also hated her because I didn't really hate her at all; I just wished that things like this could come easy to me, too. I wished I wasn't so scared. I sat staring out the window for the remainder of the hour, focusing on being jealous and annoyed at Kelly. At least if I just thought about that, I wouldn't have to think about what I was about to face at my first day of high school.

As the bus pulled into the parking lot of Adam's Prep, my phone beeped with a text from Jake.

*The homerooms r posted in front of the main office. You're in 108, and I'm in 113. I wish we could have been 2gether! I'll text you when I get my schedule 2 see if we have any classes.*

"We're in homeroom 108," I turned and told Kelly. "Jake's in 113. He said the homerooms are posted outside the main office. I wonder if any of our friends are in ours."

"Let's go check it out!" Kelly replied.

We were a little familiar with the layout of the school from our tours and eighth grade visit days, so we headed towards the main office. The hallways were overwhelming. Some of the seniors looked so old, and there had to be at least a hundred kids in every hallway we turned down. I only recognized about ten faces. The uniforms were odd too. I wore them at St. Anne's, so I was used to it, but it was still weird to see so many kids in the exact same khaki skirt or pants, white oxford shirt, and maroon sweater. I felt like I was in a creepy, life size L.L. Bean ad.

"That's weird. The homerooms are not alphabetical, just random. We're actually not in the same homeroom, Kate, because they're not organized by last names. I'm in 110. Oh look – Jada is in there with me!" Kelly smiled as she turned to get ready to head for her homeroom.

I panicked. I couldn't breathe, so I leaned back against the wall for a second. All the blood was rushing to my head, and I knew if I didn't sit down I would start to feel sick. I couldn't believe this! Kelly would not be in my homeroom with me. I had never even imagined this could happen. We were always together. From the very first day that Dad had dropped us off at preschool, Kelly had been by my side. How was I going to do this without her?

"Kate," Kelly immediately recognized my reaction and I could see a mixture of concern and dismay on her face, "you'll be fine! It's only homeroom. We still might have some classes or free periods together, and even if we don't, you're my sister – we will always be best friends!"

I closed my eyes, leaned back against the cold wall, and took a deep breath.

"You can do this, Katie." Kelly rubbed my back, "Who knows? You might even like it!"

I could do this. I *HAD* to do this, so I might as well suck it up, and get through the first day. I opened my eyes, gave Kelly a little smile, and said, "OK, you're right. Let's go."

We walked towards Freshman Hall and started to find our rooms. On the way, we ran into Gia.

"Hey guys," she said waving. "I'm in homeroom 102. None of our friends are in there, just Greg Morton, and I really don't plan on talking to him." Greg was a kind of geeky kid who went to St. Anne's with us. Gia's not the type to ignore someone just because they're not popular, but Greg was sort of an obnoxious geek. He was always reminding people how smart he was, and that his parents bought him all the coolest new gadgets. I was pretty happy when both Gopi and I had beaten him in class rank last year. He had consoled himself by buying the latest version of the Blackberry, even though it's not like anyone ever texts him anyway.

"I don't blame you," I told Gia, "I wouldn't buddy up with him either. Have you guys seen Jake?" I stood on my tippy toes to try and scan all the faces in freshman hallway. I knew he was here. Where could he have gone? It seemed weird he hadn't found me. Just as I made my mind up to start peeking in rooms to find Jake, the bell rang and the feeling of sickening dread quickly returned.

"This is it, guys," I said to Gia and Kelly. "Good luck!"

"It won't be so bad, Kate, text us if you can so we can figure out what classes we have together," Kelly said, as she gave me a quick hug.

"Bye guys, hopefully we'll have lunch," Gia said, in a quieter tone than Kelly's. She turned and headed back to her homeroom. That left just me standing alone in the hallway with people walking past me in every direction. I took a deep breath, figured out that 108 would have to be down the hall and on the left side, and headed towards my new homeroom.

I looked around for anyone I might know, and realized that I knew absolutely no one. I decided my best bet was to take a seat in the back and just fly quietly under the radar.

My homeroom teacher walked in and I was a little surprised to see that he was a guy. At St. Anne's we had only ever had older, female teachers. They were very mom-like; some were even grandmom-like, and I had liked that. I'd never had a young, male teacher before. I guess it was just another thing I would have to get used to. He introduced himself as Mr. Sewell, and he seemed pretty nice. He said he only taught Junior and Senior English, but for some reason he had been assigned a freshman homeroom.

"They're making a lot of changes this year in how they're running the homerooms," Mr. Sewell began. "Just to give you guys a heads up on how things work here, if you're out of uniform, you'll get a demerit in homeroom. You need to hold on to that demerit all day, because any other teacher who notices a uniform violation will ask if you've already received a demerit. If you can't prove that you have, they will write you another one. If you're absent, you won't be admitted into homeroom without an absent slip, and it has to be signed by the main office. If you're late, you have to go to the office to get a late slip before you come to homeroom. There are never to be any cell phones, cameras, or iPods in school. Put them in your locker when you get here, and don't take them back out. If a teacher or an administrator catches you using them, that's five demerits. Ten demerits equal an after school detention."

Mr. Sewell looked around the room at the thirty, silent, overwhelmed freshman staring straight ahead. I think he started to feel a little bad for us.

"It's really not that bad, guys. You'll all get used to it. As long as you follow the rules, respect your teachers and peers, and do your work, you'll do fine here at Adam's. Most kids end up loving it here."

His words barely consoled me, but he did seem to have a genuine smile. I guess it was a good sign that the first teacher I met seemed pretty nice, even if I wouldn't actually have him until junior or senior year.

"Oh yeah, there is one other change," Mr. Sewell interrupted my thoughts. "This year our Homeroom Representatives were picked at random, rather than being elected. Our Principal, Mr. Keeley, thought that would help to get more students involved because we tend to see the same kids participating in all the activities."

"What's a Homeroom Representative?" a red-haired girl in the front row asked.

"They're a part of the Student Council, they'll help to organize all the freshmen level events, stand on stage in the auditorium during class meetings, help to plan the Freshman Field Day. They basically help to represent your class as whole," Mr. Sewell replied.

"Who is it for our homeroom?" a boy in the back asked.

"Um, let me check," said Mr. Sewell as he ruffled through some papers in his folder.

"Ours are Marcus White and Katie McKinney."

*'Dear God, No!!!!!'* I said to myself, as I instinctively slunk into my seat, and my cheeks blazed a bright red.

"Cool," said Marcus, a tall, African American boy with an Adam's Prep Football bag leaning against his desk. "Which one of you is Katie? Isn't that Jake William's girlfriend?"

My tongue felt like it weighed a hundred pounds, and my mouth was horribly dry. As usual I was unable to say like any normal person would, *"Oh that's me! I guess you know Jake from football?"* Instead the words hung heavy in my mouth and I awkwardly stared at my desk while every head in the room swiveled around trying to figure out who Katie was, and why she wasn't responding. Somehow I got my hand to slowly raise up.

"Are you Katie?" Mr. Sewell asked. "Wow, you must be pretty shy, Kate!"

Thank you Captain Obvious, I thought. My God, could this get *ANY* worse?

## Chapter 5

In Homeroom we got our schedules and our locker combinations. First period I had Honors Algebra with Gopi, we got to talk for a few minutes, and she seemed just as nervous as I was. We only managed to chat as we walked in and out, because we sat nowhere near each other. Second period I had French, and Leslie Smith from my class last year was in there, so that was good. We weren't great friends, but any familiar face was nice to see.

Third period was lunch, and I was praying that I knew someone else who had that period free. I had been absolutely paranoid to take out my phone and text everyone to see what their schedules were like, for fear of getting caught. When I got to my locker I grabbed my phone, and just as I'd suspected, I had three new texts waiting for me. How come no one else ever seemed as scared as I was to get in trouble?

The first was from Jake:

*Yo Kates! I have lunch 3^{rd} – hope you r in there 2! How's your day so far?XOXO*

The second was from Jada, and I think she had sent it to all of us:

*Hey girlies! Isn't this awesome??? I luv it so far. U guys have to meet the soccer gurlz they are the best. Anyone else free 3?*

The last one was from Kelly:

*How u makin out Kates? I luv it here! I have lunch 4 – how bout u?*

I looked up from my phone just in time to see Jake approaching.

"I have lunch now, too!" I said, "and Jada texted me that she'll be in there too."

"Cool! See, it's not so bad? How were your classes so far?" Jake asked. "Mine were boring. I really wish I could just play football and not even go to class."

"They were OK. I have Honors Algebra with Gopi, and Leslie's in my French class. Both the teachers seemed OK," I replied, as I headed towards the cafeteria. Just then Gopi turned the corner from the other hallway.

"Hey guys! You have lunch now too?" she asked.

"Yeah, and I think Jada's in here too. This is awesome that we all have free together!" I said. I was relieved that I wouldn't have to eat alone.

We walked in and scanned the tables in the cafeteria. It seemed to be divided up pretty much by grade, so we headed over to where all the freshmen were clustered. Jake immediately recognized a few of the football players and they started shouting out his name to come and sit with them.

"Is it cool if I go over with the guys since your friends are in here too?" he turned and whispered to me.

I wanted to grab onto his arm and beg him not to leave me. I looked around at this sea of sweater vests, khaki-colored uniform pants and skirts, and unfamiliar faces, and I just wanted to take his hand, run out, and never come back. But I didn't want Jake to see that side of me. I knew if I could just get through this first day, it would get better. Or at least, I really hoped it would.

"Yeah sure," I whispered. "I'll be fine here with Gopi, and we can find Jada."

"Cool! Thanks, Kate!" he said. Then he leaned in and whispered quietly in my ear, "Love you."

With that, Jake took off to go sit next to the freshman football team. They high-fived him and slapped him on the back as he sat down. A few pointed at me. I could tell by the way Jake blushed that they were asking if I was his girlfriend.

Gopi and I looked at each other and tried to determine our next move.

"Should we get our food and try to pick out a seat while we're in line?" Gopi suggested.

"Sounds good. Maybe we'll run into Jada," I said, slowly making my way towards the crowded food lines. Gopi and I stood right beside each other, barely saying a word as I bought my turkey hoagie, fries and a soda. Gopi only bought a juice because she had brought her lunch from home. After we paid, I scanned the room one more time for Jada.

"There she is!" Gopi exclaimed pointing to Jada and a table full of girls I didn't recognize. We made our way over.

"Hey, Jada," I said, as we got closer.

Jada was laughing at something a blonde girl next to her had just whispered in her ear. "Hi guys!" she exclaimed. "I'm so happy you're in here. These are my new friends from the soccer team, Madison, Kylie and Brianna."

Gopi and I both said hi, and smiled, but the response we got back was less than friendly. The three girls looked us up and down, and slightly smiled. No one said a word. Jada started to look uncomfortable. Then I realized there were no other seats at their table, but a whole table was empty right next to them.

"We'll just sit over there," Gopi said quietly. I recognized the look on her face, as she stared down towards the floor. It was the same shy, sad look she had when she first came to St. Anne's and had no friends. For about the millionth time that day, my cheeks blazed a bright red, as I turned to sit alone at the table with Gopi. We opened our lunches and started taking a few bites. Although I was angry that Jada had let her friends treat us like that, I still fully expected her to come and sit with us. We were best friends, right? I knew Jada loved sports, and meeting new people, but some girls from the soccer team couldn't replace her best friends – right? Just as I was thinking this, I glanced up to see if Jada was coming yet.

I heard the blonde girl, Madison, say, "Ewww! Her lunch smells disgusting! What is she eating?"

She was talking about Gopi's lunch. I saw Gopi turn a bright shade of red and slide the lid back over her Tupperware. Then I saw Jada, who hadn't moved an inch to come and sit wth us, shrug her shoulders and say, "It's just the food her mom makes. It is kinda weird."

For the first time that day I felt an emotion besides nervousness and shyness. Anger overcame me. I turned and glared at Jada. How could she? I had seen her eat Mrs. Patel's food a million times and shovel it down, while saying how good it was. How could she care more what those stupid girls thought than me and Gopi? How could she leave us to sit at this table all alone?

"Kate, what do you have next period?" Jada yelled over, in an attempt to act like everything was OK.

I didn't even bother responding, I just turned around. Jada would need to do a lot more than make a casual comment to make up for this. I smiled at Gopi to make her feel better. Then I pulled my book bag up onto my lap, and reached inside.

Without letting anyone see what I was doing, I ran my fingers over the soft, tattered edges of the four-year-old card. I had turned it inside out before I hid it in my bag this morning, so that I could peek in all day and see the signature in purple pen that said, *'Happy Birthday! Love, Mom'.* I guess in a way, I was hoping that having her card would make up for not having her here today.

Right then it didn't matter that Gopi was next to me, that Jake was a few tables away, or that Jada had just hurt my feelings to hang out with some random girls. All that mattered was that again it was one of those moments when I really needed my mom, and again she wasn't there.

She had never, ever been there when I needed her. I missed her so badly at that moment that it literally hurt.

I pulled my hand out of the bag and forced myself to put it back under the table. Then I sat at the table staring ahead at all the laughing faces, pushing my food around on my tray, and making small talk with Gopi. How was it that with so many people around me, it was still possible

to feel so alone?

## Chapter 6

The sand felt warm under my arms and on the inch or so of skin that was showing between my shirt and pants. I hadn't even bothered with a blanket today. I was in such a rush to get out of school and get down to the lake. I needed peace and quiet to think. A blanket to lie on had been the last thing on my mind. It didn't matter though, I liked the feel of the hot sand, and I could take a nice, hot shower when I was done. *If* I was ever done being at the lake; it seemed like a pretty nice idea to stay here forever and never go back to school again.

I sat up a little and dipped my toe into the edge of the brown water. It was nice and cool. I tipped my head back, pulled the headband out of my hair, and let the sun warm my face. The day's events started to run though my head again. Kelly and I weren't in the same homeroom, I was going to have to be the Homeroom Representative, Jake had already made friends with the whole freshman football team, Jada sat with those awful girls that made fun of Gopi in the cafeteria, and then one of them, Madison, ended up being in my gym class. The whole day was a blur of bells, hallways, books, and unfamiliar faces.

Kelly was still at school because she was trying out for cheerleading, Jada was at soccer practice and Jake was at football practice. They were all fitting in so easily. Why was it so hard for me? I wished I didn't always feel so nervous, so alone. Maybe if I were more outgoing like my sister, I could enjoy things more. Maybe that's why she was able to forget about mom and I never was. Kelly doesn't need Mom. She's smart, pretty, a great dancer, and she always has someone to talk to, or be close to.

She makes friends so easily. For the second time that day, I hated Kelly. But I only hated her because I wanted to be more like her.

I pulled my feet out of the water, stretched my arms and legs out, and fell asleep under the sun. I felt exhausted, maybe because we hadn't had much sleep the night of our sleepover or because I had lain awake for nights worrying about school starting. Maybe it was because I had to wake up this morning at practically the crack of dawn, or maybe the stress of the day had just made me tired. Whatever the reason, I found it easy to finally relax now that I was at my spot at the lake, and a few minutes after I lay down, I was sound asleep.

I woke up to a text beeping on my phone:

*U at the lake? Come 2 the house – I have big news!*

It was from Kelly; I guessed that her news was that she made the freshman cheerleading team. As much as I didn't want to, I decided it probably was time to head in to the house, plus I wanted to see if Jake was home yet, so we could talk. I stood up, brushed as much of the sand off of me as I could, and headed home.

Kelly practically jumped on me as I walked through the door.

"Guess what?" She yelled excitedly.

"You made the cheerleading team?"

"I didn't just make the team, Kates, I made JV! Only two freshman girls were picked to move up and I was one of them!" I could see how happy Kelly was, and even though I'd been feeling horribly jealous of her lately, I was still happy for her. I leaned over and gave her a big hug.

"That's awesome, Kell, I'm so excited for you!" I forced myself to say. "How did you get on JV?"

"I lucked out. You know I have no idea how to do stunts or any of the gymnastic moves, but all they did for tryouts was teach us a really complex dance number that they want to use at half time this year, and I did it really well! I was so lucky they happened to pick the dance as what they focused on for tryouts!" Kelly was smiling from ear to ear as she told me about the tryouts and popped Pringles into her mouth.

"I guess I can't eat these anymore," she laughed and put the can back up onto the shelf. "You would not believe how tiny those skirts are, Kate. I'm going to have to live on carrots and apples to look good in them."

I know my sister expected me to tell her not to worry and that she would look great no matter what, but all I could think about was all of the perfect, beautiful cheerleaders jumping up and down, doing flips and dancing in front of Jake every day after school in those tiny little skirts. The sick feeling started to return to my stomach. I tried to count in my head exactly how many days it was until football season was over. *Hmmm, about 30 days in a month, like 3 months of football, but September had already started…………..*

"Girls! How did it go?" Luckily, I was interrupted by Dad entering the kitchen with a huge smile on his face, "Did you like it?"

"Oh my God, Dad, it was awesome!" Kelly said as she started into practically a minute-by-minute recount of her entire day for Dad. "My homeroom teacher, Miss Wilson, is really nice. She's young, and has long, black hair and blue eyes, she seems so cool – I can't even believe she's a teacher. And guess what? I have her for Algebra I, too. My Science teacher and my Spanish teacher seem nice too, and I didn't know anyone in my free, but I sat with some girls from Washington Township that I had seen before at dance competitions and they were really cool. Oh and Jada's in my gym class and my Lit class……"

I got annoyed again as Kelly rambled on a mile a minute about how perfect her day had been.

Finally, Dad interrupted her, "Wait, I haven't heard you mention anything about Katie at all in your day. Don't you guys have any classes together?" he asked.

"Not one. Not even homeroom." It was the first thing I'd said at all about school. I wanted Dad to recognize the pouty look I put on my face.

"Oh it's really not a big deal, Dad. Kate exaggerates. We're on the bus together every morning and we *LIVE* together. I think we can handle not spending every waking moment at school together."

My chest tightened, and my eyes start to sting. How could Kelly feel that way? I wanted so badly to be with her during the day, and she was happy not to have to be around me? We're sisters! Twin sisters! Aren't we supposed to be best friends? Kelly didn't even notice that what she said had hurt me. Why did I always have to be the sensitive one? She kept going with the story of her perfect day.

"Anyway, Dad, I didn't even get to tell you the best part yet," Kelly said, as I slumped into a chair at the table. "I made the cheerleading team!"

"That's great, sweetie!" Dad gave Kelly a hug.

"I know!" she exclaimed, "And I didn't just make the team, I am one of only two freshman who made JV."

"Kelly, that really is impressive. I'm proud of you," Dad said. "I bet you're going to make an excellent cheerleader."

I had heard just about enough about how wonderful Kelly's first day of school had been. I leaned on my elbow and started folding a napkin into a tiny little triangle.

"Of course she'll make a great cheerleader," I said. Kelly turned to me with a smile, but I couldn't stop myself, even though I knew I would ruin her moment. "Mom was a cheerleader too. Grandma said she was Captain of the squad, so I guess it's in your blood, Kell."

As soon as I said it, I regretted it. I had only meant to make Kelly stop talking about her stupid day, but I didn't think about what it would do to Dad. Every time Mom's name was mentioned you could literally see how badly it hurt him. His eyes seemed distant, and he would stare right past you, as his hand gripped onto something, and his knuckles turned white. Then the few seconds where he looked like he was going to cry would pass, and a different look would quickly come over his face, an angry one.

The smile wiped off Kelly's face as well.

"Nice, Kate," she said," You really just can't resist bringing her up, can you?"

I really could have cared less about hurting Kelly, but she was right, I felt horrible for upsetting Dad.

"I'm sorry," I mumbled and let the hair fall over the side of my face so that I didn't have to look at him. Dad took off his glasses and rubbed the bottom of his forehead right between his eyes. He was quiet for a minute.

"It's OK, Katie, you didn't mean anything by it. And you're right; she was a cheerleader and a very good one." He replaced his glasses and forced a smile, "How does meatloaf sound for dinner tonight?"

The problem was, I had meant it, and I felt horrible for hurting him. And I hated that I felt guilty for being jealous of Kelly and wanted to ruin her moment too. Just because I'd had a bad first day of school didn't mean I had to take it out on my family. I needed to snap out of it.

"Meatloaf's OK with me," I said. "I'm gonna go upstairs and IM Jake. I'll be down in half an hour."

So I did. I went upstairs, chatted with Jake on the computer, pretended to be thrilled when I heard that he too had made JV. I acted as if my first day hadn't been completely horrendous, and I was just like any other kid who was excited to be starting high school. I went downstairs, ate my meatloaf, took a shower, and pretended to be super tired. Then I crawled into my soft, comfy bed, wanting not to think about any of it, and just go to sleep.

Before I went up though, I made sure to grab my book bag, so I could slip the birthday card back under my pillow – I still couldn't sleep without it.

## Chapter 7

I lay on top of Gopi's pink, flowered comforter next to my sister and looked around the room. It was the first time the five of us were having a sleepover since the night before school started. I was happy to be there, but in these few weeks so much has changed. Gopi and I have grown really close. We have almost all our classes together, we study together, and together we can't stand Madison DiCicco. Somehow, Madison has become a good friend of Jada and Kelly's, yet never misses a chance to scowl in disgust or roll her eyes at me and Gopi. I barely ever actually see Gia, but we talk every night. She seems very uninterested in school. I know she isn't doing too well with her grades, except for Art class of course, and she hasn't made many friends. She doesn't seem to care though. According to her, as long as she has us, she doesn't need anyone else in the school. Even though I barely see her during the day, I know Gia is still one of my close, close friends.

I'm worried though, that things are heating up again between her parents. It seems like the worse their fighting gets, the more withdrawn Gia becomes. She's been painting a lot lately, and I saw an amazing picture she drew hanging up in her locker. Whenever Gia turns to her artwork, it's usually because she wants to escape away from something bothering her. She deals with her problems by focusing on her art, in her own little world. Her room, with its little side studio, is a lot like the lake is for me. And lately, I had certainly been spending my fair share of time down at the lake.

Actually though, I've been doing pretty well dealing with all the changes I've been going through. It has been exactly a month since school started, and I'm getting a lot better at handling everything. Jake and I have managed to stay close, even though it seems like he is one of the most popular boys in the freshman class. A lot of girls always say how cute he is, and almost all the guys want to be friends with him, but he is still my sweet Jake. He calls me every night, texts me during the day, and we even have plans to go to the shore tomorrow for our anniversary. I'm really excited to get to spend the whole day with him.

Other things are getting better too. I ride the bus every morning and afternoon without wincing now. I'm able to concentrate on my homework, instead of worrying about the kids around me that I don't know. I'm used to my schedule, my classes, and my teachers. I have A's in all of my classes, even though I got 70 on my last History quiz. I have most of my classes with Gopi, and she helps me to stay focused on my grades. I've even made a few new friends in some of my classes. No one has mentioned a word about the Homeroom Reps having to do anything, so I'm hoping maybe they just forgot about that whole initiative, and I won't ever have to stand up and represent room 108.

Jada has started sitting with us at lunch again, even though she usually gets up and disappears for twenty minutes to go and talk to her soccer friends. I don't mind so much now though; I know she needs to be friends with the girls on the team. The only one that really bothers me is Madison, but it seems like everyone besides Gopi and I think she's great. Kelly certainly likes her, and even worse, so does Jake. They ended up being lab partners in Biology and he insists she's a really nice girl. UGH!

But besides that, things really aren't too bad. I've gotten over the first few days, which are definitely the worst, and I know now that even if I don't like high school that much, I'll get through it. I've even been able to stop hiding the birthday card from Mom in my bag every day, and most days I'm doing alright without it. I've stopped feeling so jealous of Kelly too, and started loving having my twin sister again. I looked over at her and smiled, thinking how lucky I was to have her, and the fact that she always puts up with all my worries and stuff.

"Katie, why are you giving me that goofy smile?" Kelly laughed and threw a pink pillow that hit me directly in the head.

I laughed too and threw one back, "Sorry, I was just thinking about stuff."

"Shocker!" Jada said teasingly, "Katie, thinking about stuff – imagine that!"

"Sorry," I said shrugging my shoulders, "You guys know I can't help it, I always get caught up just thinking about stuff. Like right now as I got nailed in the head with a pink pillow, lying on a pink bed, with a pink teddy, I was thinking, 'Wow! Gopi has an amazingly lot of pink stuff in her room!' Seriously, Gop, you even have a pink hamper!" Honestly, every single item in Gopi's room was decorated pink.

"Gopi," Gia asked, "I thought your favorite color was green?"

"It is," she replied. "Why?"

"Then why is everything in your room so incredibly pink? Pink comforter, pink sheets, pink rug, pink border, pink curtains, pink walls; there are seriously like nine different shades of pink in this room and you don't even like the color," Gia replied.

"You wouldn't understand," she shrugged her shoulders.

"Understand what, Gop?" Jada asked, "Why you don't like pink?"

"No, pink is a color that's for girls. Girls are supposed to like pink, so my parents have gotten me everything in pink since the day I was born. It doesn't matter that I don't like it, they're just things. Having a lot of pink things is kinda the least of my worries."

"If your favorite color is green," Kelly asked, "Why don't you just tell them that?"

"You don't get it, Kell. My parents are different from your Dad. When you're a Muslim girl, that's all you're ever supposed to be. A well behaved, obedient, girl who loves and respects her parents and one day will do the same for her husband."

I recognized the look of discomfort on Gopi's face. I knew it was hard for her to have to try and explain her family's culture and beliefs. People always made it seem so horrible that Gopi's mom and dad had so many rules, but really it wasn't. They were just doing what they thought was best for her because the loved her. Plus their strictness had gotten her older sister, Abhaya, into Yale, so it couldn't be all that bad.

Gopi was still trying to explain to everyone, "They just see me as their perfect little girl, who likes sweet, cute, little, pink things."

"Your husband! I'm not getting married till I'm like 35," Jada said popping a chip into her mouth. "Plus why are you so worried about upsetting your parents, if you like green, just tell them you like green." She shrugged and searched around the bowl for a chip that was folded over. Those were Jada's favorite kind because she claimed they were the crunchiest. She always picked all the folded over chips out of the bowl.

"I just don't think it's worth disappointing them and having an argument over. If I'm going to do that, I'd rather argue for something that's worth it, like being allowed to go to the football game this Friday. I would much rather see Trey Williams in those tight uniform pants, than fight over pink curtains!" Gopi giggled and everyone else joined in.

"Trey is so hot! If Jake looks like him when he's a senior, watch out, Katie!" Jada teased.

I laughed. Jake and Trey actually didn't look that much alike, besides their blue eyes. Jake was blonde and tall, and Trey had black hair and was much shorter, even though he was four years older. I had to admit though, Trey was pretty cute.

"I have such a crush on him, it's not even funny," Jada said. "He actually talked to me when I was leaving practice the other day, it was awesome!"

"What did he say?" Kelly asked.

"He just asked my name and if I was a freshman. And he said he heard I was pretty good at soccer. Do you think I should try friending him on Facebook?"

"Do it!" Gia said, "Why not?"

"What if he rejects me?" For the first time ever, Jada seemed uncertain of herself.

"Are you crazy, Jada?!" Kelly exclaimed. "You're beautiful, and nice, and funny, and no one is going to reject you as a friend!"

"Seriously," said Gopi, "If I were allowed to have a Facebook, I would friend a cute, senior guy who had talked to me."

"Alright, I'll do it," Jada said smiling. "Now let's watch that movie."

"No," Kelly jumped in the conversation, "before we put in any movies we *HAVE* to talk about Friday night. It's like the biggest game of the year. It's going to be so much fun and I think we're gonna kill Lenape."

"I'm definitely going," Jada said, while she crunched on her latest chip, "the whole girls' soccer team is going together."

"Then who are we supposed to go with if Kelly's cheering at the game and Jada's going with her team?" I asked.

"The three of us can go together. I think I can actually convince my parents to let me go because it's a school sponsored event, and I'll be with my girlfriends," Gopi said.

"Awesome, you can actually go!" I gave her a high five. "Gia will you come with us?"

Gopi and I both gave her our biggest smiles, "C'mon Gi, it'll be fun!" Gopi pleaded.

"I don't really see anything about high school football that's fun," Gia said, "idiotic, over-hyped, and a pure jock fest maybe, but not fun."

I started to panic that it would just be Gopi and me amongst the hundreds of people in the crowd. Or worse yet, that we'd have to sit with Jada and Madison would be there, but then I saw Gia's familiar, impish grin start to form on her face.

"But I guess if you guys really want to inflate the already ginormous egos of the obnoxious, South Jersey, sports-driven boys we go to school with, I'll be there," Gia said with a sarcastic, yet hilarious, tone.

"Yeah!" Gopi and I said, reaching over to hug her.

"Who knows, Gi, they may even serve vegan hot dogs,"
I joked.

Everybody laughed, and I was actually kind of excited
about my first weekend event at Adam's Prep.

"*Now* can we put the movie in?" Jada asked, and she
popped in yet another one of her scary movies that she
loved. Gopi looked to make sure the door was locked,
probably because she knew her mom would not approve
of an R-rated movie, Gia took out a bottle of dark blue nail
polish and started to paint her toes to match her fingers,
and Kelly came and laid next to me on the big pink pillow
to watch the movie. I looked around again at the five of us,
and thought that maybe things weren't so different after
all. Maybe after the first few months everything would go
back to being the same between us, and the five of us
could actually enjoy the next four years together. I smiled
thinking of this, and of the date Jake and I had for

tomorrow, and thought that things were definitely getting a lot better.

### Chapter 8

The sand felt warm underneath our blanket, and the
seagulls squawked over our heads, as wave after wave
rolled up and onto the shore. The sky was bright blue and
almost cloudless. It was an amazingly warm day for the
last weekend in September, and I had no use for the
sweatshirt I had packed for our day trip to the beach. I did,
however, wish that I would have packed some of the
snacks I had wanted to bring with us, but left at home in
an attempt to try and look as skinny as the cheerleaders
that Jake was always surrounded by. The delicious smells
drifting down from the boardwalk were making me
incredibly hungry. I thought that since it was fall most of

the boardwalk would be shut down, but apparently in Wildwood most of the stores and restaurants stay open through October and the familiar scents of popcorn, pizza and cotton candy were driving me crazy.

"What are you thinking about, Katie?" Jake asked as he sat up on the blanket and looked down at me.

I laughed.

"Well, actually, food," I replied.

Jake started laughing too.

"Food?" he said smiling. "Usually when you get all quiet on me you're either nervous about something, going over something you need to memorize for a test, or thinking about a situation with you and your friends, but I don't think I've ever heard you say you were laying there thinking about like cheese steaks and fruit snacks before," he teased.

"Well," I smiled playfully at him, "that's because I usually just eat if I'm hungry, but in an attempt to have a perfect body like the rest of the girls at Adam's Prep, eating is a habit I've tried to give up! And BTW, Jake, I don't really care for cheese steaks or fruit snacks; they're both your favorites."

"That's cause they're the most delicious foods in the world," Jake joked. "I guess that pizza must be pretty tempting right now then, huh?" Then he playfully poked his finger into my side to make me laugh. "I know how much you love pizza. Remember at Tim's graduation party when you ate like four slices?"

"Haha! Shut up! I was really hungry from swimming all day!" I said rolling away from him, even though I liked how close he had moved to me on the blanket. "That pizza does happen to smell really, really good right now though."

"Then let me buy you some lunch, because you're beautiful, Katie, and the last thing you need to be worried about is how you look. Believe me, all I ever hear about from the guys on the football team is how good looking you are."

"Really?" I asked. I was shocked that they found me attractive.

"Yeah all the time," Jake said, "but I hate it because I know if we ever break up, they are going to be all over you."

I turned my head to look right at him, "I thought we were never going to break up?" I asked.

I listened closely to hear his answer; partly because since we started high school I didn't feel quite as close to Jake as I had before, and partly because I just liked to hear him tell me we would be together forever.

"We aren't," he said and gently kissed me on the lips. "Now how about that lunch?"

"OK," I held his hand as we walked up the beach towards the boardwalk. We headed straight for Mac's Pizza and got some Cokes and a few slices. As I bit down into the first, hot, cheesy bite Jake started to talk about school, which was the last thing I wanted to think about right then.

"I can't believe we didn't end up in any classes together," Jake said, "at least I get to see you in lunch."

"Yeah I mainly have classes with Gopi. I think it's because we're both in Honors classes. I don't really see Kelly or the other girls during the day either."

"Well at least you can sneak in a text or two to them in the halls. I swear girls can get away with anything at that school, and I have Mr. Summers on me like a hawk constantly. He's already taken my phone twice this year. I think all he does all day is stand in the halls waiting for kids to do something wrong."

I laughed. "You don't exactly try to hide it when you text, Jake. Both times he took it you were walking right down the hall with your phone in your hand! You have to like lean into your locker and text, or hide the phone under a book."

Jake laughed too, "Whatever, even if you're right, I swear that guy loves to bust my balls. You think they'd be happy to have some good football players at that school. They haven't won a homecoming game in the past three years."

"Wow, somebody's getting a little cocky!" I teased, "I guess I didn't know what an amazing gift of a football player Jake Williams was to Adam's Prep High School!"

Jake blushed. "Sorry, I didn't mean it like that. I think I am going to dress for Varsity though at the game Friday night. Isn't that awesome?" he asked.

"Yeah, it's really cool! Do you think you'll get to play at all?"

"I doubt it. We're playing Lenape, and they're a huge school, so their team's really good. It's kinda cool though just to get to sit with the team. Trey didn't dress for Varsity until last year when he was a junior. My dad is psyched," Jake said.

It was obvious how excited he was for the game. The thought of having to play a Varsity level sport against seniors from other schools would have made me a nervous wreck, but Jake loved the challenge.

"You'll be there, right?" he asked, taking my hand to hold in his.

"I'll definitely be there," I promised him, "Gopi, Gia and I are going to go together."

Jake paid the bill and then took my hand again to walk out of the restaurant. We strolled along the boardwalk and

I looked at all the familiar sights: the white loops of the tallest coaster that loomed up in the sky and sat directly above the ocean below, the millions of colored lights from the piers that glistened in the sunlight even when they weren't lit up, the stuffed animals, balloons and electronics that lined the back rows of the games, and rack after rack of jewelry, clothes and sunglasses that spilled out of the stores and onto the boards. I loved being down the shore, I closed my eyes for a second and breathed in the smell of the ocean mixed with the scents of the boardwalk food.

"Was this an OK place to spend our anniversary?" Jake asked. "I know how much you love the beach."

"It was perfect!" I said, squeezing his hand a little tighter.

"Wanna play a game?" Jake asked, and he pulled me over to one of the games where you shoot a stream of water to make your horse race faster.

"Only if you want to lose!" I teased. "It just so happens that I'm an expert at this game!"

"Bring it on, Katie!"

The announcer took money from us and from two little boys who sat down next to us to play. Then he rang the buzzer for the race to begin. I focused on the little red dot in the center of my target until I heard the announcer yell, "Horse number four! We have a winner!"

"That's me!" I yelled, jumping from my seat.

"Wow, you are really good at this," Jake laughed.

"Thanks," I said smiling, "go ahead, pick any prize you want."

"Me? Don't you want the prize?"

"Nah, I have a million stuffed animals. You can have it," I said.

"I'll take the Spongebob doll," Jake said to the man. I thought it was a little odd he picked this. They had DVDs you could pick and giant boxes of candy, both of which I thought Jake would like. I had no idea why he would pick a stuffed Spongebob. Then I saw him walk over to the little boys who had been playing next to us and hand them the surprise. Yep, it was official, my boyfriend was just about the sweetest guy ever, and I really, really loved him.

When Jake came back I leaned in and gave him a kiss, "That was really sweet."

"It was nothing," he shrugged. "Wanna go on the Ferris wheel?"

Jake grabbed my hand again and ran towards Mariners Pier. Since it was September and daytime, there was no one waiting in line to go on the ride. We got on right away, and it slowly began circling around.

"Look there's the Frisbee toss where that guy from Cherry Hill tried to impress Kelly with the giant, stuffed lion," I pointed out laughing.

"I think it must have worked, Kate, because if I remember right she spent the entire night with him," Jake replied.

"True," I laughed, "and look there's where you and Rob were skin boarding that day my dad took us all down the shore. Remember how many times you wiped out?"

"Hey, the surf was rough that day. It wasn't my fault!" Jake was laughing too.

As we rounded the top, our car stopped at the very top spot. I looked out and over the ocean. Jake gently put his hand on my cheek and started kissing me. We kissed there for a minute, at the top of the world, until our car started moving again and began its slow descent down.

When we got off the Ferris wheel, the sun was starting to get lower and the first shades of pink, orange and purple appeared in the sky.

"Wanna split an ice cream before we leave?" Jake asked.

"Sure."

We walked down to Baskin Robins and Jake told me to wait outside on the bench while he went in and got us our sundae. I kicked off my flip flops, curled my legs up against my chest, and leaned my head back to catch the last few rays of sunlight. I loved the way they warmed my face. I hadn't felt this happy or relaxed for a long time.

"Here you go Katie," I heard Jake say. I opened my eyes expecting to see a mountain of ice cream and whipped topping, but instead there was a small, shiny white box with a big, blue bow.

"Oh my god, Jake, I didn't know you were getting me a present! Today was present enough!"

"I wanted to. Open it!" I could hear the excitement in his voice, as I took the box out of his hand and unwrapped it.

Inside was a single, small, silver chain with an emerald in the shape of a heart dangling from it.

"It's so beautiful," I said. I was stunned, flattered and excited all at the same time.

"I thought it would match your green eyes," Jake said. He always noticed that they were green, not blue. "I've had it in my bag all day, but I didn't know how to get it out to give to you without ruining the surprise."

"I love it, Jake, thank you."

"So it's better than ice cream?" Jake asked.

"A million times better," I smiled in reply.

"I love you," he said and kissed me again.

Just then Jake's phone beeped with a text from his mom that she was done cleaning at their shore house and was ready to drive us home. Mrs. Williams picked us up and asked if I liked my necklace.

"It's beautiful," I said.

"I helped him pick it out. I hope you like it," she said with a smile. Jake's mom had to be one of the nicest people in the world.

"I love it," I said. "Thank you both so much."

The rest of the drive we chatted about school, football and what was going on at St. Anne's this year. Jake still had a sister in sixth grade there. Mrs. Williams told us about the colleges she was taking Trey to see, and some other funny stories from the doctor's office where she worked. Before I knew it, we were pulling into my driveway.

I just gave Jake a wave goodbye, since we were in the car with his mom, and thanked her again. When I got out of the car I saw Dad on the old porch swing with Miss Linda. He must have been waiting for me to get home. I practically jumped up the steps and onto the porch; I was still so excited about everything that had happened that day.

"How was it, Kiddo?" Dad asked.

"It was perfect," I replied. And it was. It had been an absolutely perfect day. I fingered the tiny emerald on my necklace and ran upstairs to tell Kelly all about it.

**Chapter 9**

The game on Friday night and the upcoming

Homecoming Dance were all anybody talked about the

entire week. It was odd overhearing so many people

talking about Jake, when they had no idea I even knew

him. I was trying hard to still concentrate on my school

work and not to think too much about all the social stuff

going on. Quarter 1 was going to end in three weeks, and

I really wanted to make First Honors. I still got nervous

about going to things at Adam's because there were so

many unfamiliar faces, but I actually was starting to get a

little excited to see Jake play in the big game, and I was

definitely excited for the Homecoming Dance in a few weeks.

Gopi and I were changing for Gym class and discussing our plans for Friday in the old, smelly locker rooms next to the gym. Gym class was one of my least favorite times of the day, not just because of the awkward changing in a room full of strangers, or because of my complete lack of athletic skill, but mainly because Madison DiCicco was in that class. She seemed to like nothing more than to make it glaringly obvious that Gopi and I were not cool enough to be her friends, despite the fact that she had no problem hanging out with my twin sister, or my boyfriend.

"I can't believe my parents are actually letting me go to the game Friday night," Gopi said excitedly, "I'm still kind of scared they might suggest they come along though."

We both laughed, Dr. Patel was famous for suggesting that he chaperone any event he felt uncomfortable with Gopi attending, that way she could go, and he would still know she was OK. It was the only way that Gopi had been able to go to our Eighth Grade Dinner Dance.

"Well, if he does come, it's no big deal. Plenty of parents come to watch the games, it won't seem weird. I'm sure Mr. and Mrs. Williams will be there," I offered, trying to make her feel more comfortable.

Just then I noticed that Madison had been staring at us, and it instantly made me feel uncomfortable. I started attempting to put my gym shirt on over my other shirt, and pull the bottom one out without having to show my stomach, which wasn't nearly as perfect as Madison's. Gopi noticed her watching us too, and she started to speak in a much lower tone.

"No, I was just kidding," she said, "I actually know for a fact that he has to work the night shift, so we're OK – no Dr.Patel at the football game."

Our whispering hadn't worked; Madison couldn't resist the urge to butt in.

"You're worried about your parents coming to the game with you, Gopi?" she asked. "Isn't it kinda weird for your parents to want to come with you to a Friday night football game?"

"They have a lot of rules," was the only response Gopi offered her.

I butted in hoping to defend my friend, "That's why Gopi's sister was as successful as she was. She goes to Yale you know." God, I hated how uncomfortable Madison managed to make me feel. Why could she never just leave us alone?

"Can you even afford Yale when you work at Dunkin Donuts?" Madison asked in a mockingly innocent voice.

"What are you talking about?" Gopi said, "My sister doesn't work at Dunkin Donuts, she works at the library at her school."

"No, silly!" Madison said, cracking up hysterically, "Your dad! How can he afford to pay for Yale when he works at Dunkin Donuts?"

My face turned a bright red and anger started to rush through me, as I realized the deliberately cruel, racial joke that Madison just made about Gopi's father. I saw Gopi turn around and stand up as tall as her small frame would allow, and she stared Madison right in the face.

"My father does not work at a Dunkin Donuts," she said in short, harsh words.

"Oh," Madison smiled her nasty grin, "I'm sorry, 7 – Eleven, then?"

For the second time since school began, my anger started to overcome my nerves, and I stood up as tall as Gopi, right behind her, desperately thinking of the meanest possible thing I could say back, but my efforts were halted when Miss Warner, the young, athletic gym teacher that Madison always sucked up to, stepped around the corner of the lockers and right in front of Madison.

"I just happened to overhear your conversation girls," she said in a tone that was far from her normal friendly voice, "for your information, Madison, Gopi's father is a doctor. A Cardiologist to be exact, in fact, he happens to be the Cardiologist who operated on my father when he had a heart attack last year."

For the first time ever I saw Madison's face fall. This time she was the one blushing furiously and staring at the floor, and it wasn't over yet, Miss Warner kept going.

"What you just said, Miss DiCicco, was not only rude, racist, and inappropriate, it's also against our school's diversity policy. So you can change back out of your gym uniform, and head straight to Mr. Summer's office because I'm writing you up for disrespect to another student."

I couldn't believe it! Madison had finally been put in her place! I saw Gopi's face break into a smile, and I thought about how good it must feel to her after all these years of being the "different" one to finally come out on top. I instantly took back all the times I had rolled my eyes in my head when Miss Warner had us do sit ups, or run laps, and I decided she was a pretty cool teacher, even if I did hate gym. I resolved to pay her back by being the best dodge-ball and pillow hockey player I could be for the rest of the year. This wasn't saying much, but at the very least I would smile and be pleasant from here on out.

After feeling like Gopi and I had finally had our triumph over Madison, the rest of the week went by pretty quickly. Before I knew it, it was Friday night and I was getting ready for the game. Kelly had been practicing her dance routine for half time over and over. She was only on the JV squad, but apparently at home games they get to perform with the Varsity, so she was going crazy practicing. I also suspected she must have a new guy she had a crush on because she kept texting and going on the computer constantly. This wasn't odd for Kelly at all, but she was acting very secretive about it. She kept shutting her door, and keeping her phone in her pocket. This usually meant she was head over heels for whoever her man of the moment was. I wasn't too concerned; I figured I'd find out soon enough who the mystery man was since the Homecoming Dance was coming up.

Jake was excited to be dressing for the game, and he thought he might even get in for a few plays because the starting running back was out with a torn ligament. On Wednesday, he'd officially asked me to the Homecoming Dance, and I couldn't wait. After how perfect our afternoon in Wildwood had been, I knew it would be an awesome night.

Jada was bouncing off the walls because after she'd friended Trey on Facebook, he'd asked for her number and started texting her every night. He'd even specifically asked if she was going tonight and said maybe they could meet up afterwards.

I was in my room getting dressed and trying to decide what would look cute, but not be freezing for the game, when Kelly jumped in dressed in her cheerleading uniform.

"How do I look?" she said, turning in circle.

Her hair was up in her standard high ponytail, and she had curled it to make it look extra cute. The maroon and silver short skirt flattered her long, muscular legs, and the bright white sneakers she wore added the perfect touch. Even her makeup was flawless, and she had drawn a tiny, sparkly, maroon star right on her cheek that looked adorable.

"You look great," I said. Then I decided to tease her about the new crush I suspected she had, "Is there a certain football player you're trying to impress?"

Kelly got a weird look on her face and just shrugged her shoulders, "No, of course not," she replied.

I figured based on her weird reaction that she wasn't sure about this guy. Or maybe she wasn't sure if he liked her, but she definitely didn't seem like she wanted to open up about it, so I dropped the subject.

"Good luck tonight," I said, reaching over to give her a hug.

"You too," she said, "I mean, I know these things kind of make you nervous. You'll be OK, right?"

"Yeah, I'll be OK," I assured her. "I have Gopi and Gia, and then the five of us can meet up afterwards, right?"

"Right," she said, "I think some people are going out, so maybe we can all go. And I promise, no Madison."

After I had told Kelly about the incident this week with Gopi, even she thought Madison had taken it too far.

"Cool," I said, as a car horn beeped outside. One of the senior girls from the squad was here to pick Kelly up.

"OK, see you there!" she yelled, as she ran out of my room and downstairs. I turned back to the mirror and decided to apply some makeup of my own. Maybe I wouldn't be wearing a sparkly maroon star, but I could still manage to look pretty cute when I tried to. I added some blush, eye shadow, and lip gloss. Then I checked how I looked in the mirror. As a last thought, I yanked off the hoodie I had been planning to wear and put on a tight, pink sweater that matched my makeup. I glanced one last time in the mirror, and I was pretty happy with the outcome.

"*Let's do this,*" I said to myself, feeling more confident than usual. I glanced down at the picture of my mom, debated taking a minute to think about her, then decided that tonight, I didn't need her. For once, Katie McKinney was just fine on her own, and I really liked that feeling.

## Chapter 10

Gopi, Gia and I were squeezed onto the cold, metal bleachers near the very top of the home side where all the freshmen sat. It was the fourth quarter and Adam's Prep was losing to Lenape 21-7, but everyone in the crowd was still having fun. I was a little nervous being around all these people, but I was seated right between two of my best friends and the atmosphere was actually kind of exciting. I had no idea why exactly people seemed to care quite so much about high school football, but they sure did. There were fans there who had graduated years ago and just wanted to come back to see the game. Parents were there, teachers, administration, and almost every student. I may have been happy that I wasn't feeling too nervous, and I may have been excited to see Jake dress varsity, but I didn't think I would ever understand the obsession that people seemed to have with high school football.

Kelly had done well during the cheerleading team's half-time show, and Jake had gotten in for a few minutes during the third quarter. I had absolutely no idea whether he'd done well or not, because the purpose of a running back in football was still a mystery to me, but I was guessing he had done something right because when I ran into Mrs. Williams at the snack stand she'd asked if I'd seen Jake's play and she seemed pretty proud. I was proud of him too, even if I didn't understand the game of football, and it was kind of exciting to be the girlfriend of one of the guys on the team.

Jada came bounding up the stairs and over to us from where she had been sitting with the soccer team.

"A couple of girls from the team are gonna go out after the game, and Trey's gonna be there, so Jake probably will too. Do you guys wanna come?" Jada asked. The excitement was evident on her face.

"Where are we gonna go? Like Applebees or something?" I asked.

Jada let out a sigh as if I had just asked the dumbest question in the world, "No, Kate, this is high school now, we're going to a party."

"Who's party?" Gia asked.

"Lauren Towson, she's a junior, her best friend is on the soccer team with me, Chelsea Monforto."

"We don't even know these people," I interrupted, "Are you sure we're even invited?"

Jada again gave me a look as if I had absolutely no clue as to how the social functioning of high school went, and I was trying her patience with my questions.

"Katie, it's not like that. It's a *high school* party; everyone brings people and there are tons of people there. We should be excited that even though we're freshmen, we still heard about it."

"There's no way I can go," Gopi said. "You guys have fun though."

"I don't know if I want to go either," Gia said, "I probably won't know anyone there."

Jada looked pleadingly at me; in hopes that I would be the one member of her friends who would make what she seemed to think was the blatantly obvious decision. I was torn; I felt the same as Gia about being at a party with a bunch of people I didn't even know. I knew my nerves would be an absolute mess, and I probably wouldn't have the least bit of fun. At the same time though, I also knew that Jake was going, and the thought of him going without me made me even more uncomfortable than my nerves.

"If I go, Gia, would you go too? We can leave if it's too awkward."

Gia thought for a second, "I guess I don't really want to sit at home while my parents argue," she shrugged, "so I'll go with you."

I turned to Gopi, "Do you care if we go?"

"No, not at all, I have to go right home after the game anyway. Just promise you'll tell me all about it!" she said with a smile.

Gopi was truly an amazing friend. I gave her a big smile and promised I would IM her the second I got home.

"It's set then!" Jada said smiling from ear to ear, "This is gonna be an awesome night!"

After the game ended, I rushed down the bleachers and over to the side of the field to try and talk to Jake. He noticed me and waved. Then he hurried over.

"Did you see my play?" he asked excitedly.

"You were great!" I smiled shyly at him.

Jake blushed. He was smiling, and he looked oddly cute in his sweaty uniform.

"Hey there's a party at this girl Lauren's house. The whole team is going, would you want to come?"

"I'm already going," I said. I was happy to be able to say that I actually had been invited too.

"Williams, get over here!" the coach yelled.

"Awesome, I'll see you there!" Jake said as he hurried back over to his team.

Gia was waiting for me by the concession stand, and we walked over to the group of soccer girls that Jada was standing with. I was relieved to see that Madison was not one of them. We jammed into the back of some girl's car. All of the girls from the soccer team seemed to be really good friends and Jada fit right in with them. They were laughing and singing along to the song playing from someone's iPod. It was obvious that Gia and I were the odd ones out, and my shyness started to come over me. Maybe going to this party wasn't such a good idea.

When we pulled up to the house I couldn't believe how many cars were actually there. There must have been at least a hundred kids at this house, and more were still coming. Nothing could have prepared me for what I saw when I came in though. I don't know why I'm always so naïve, but for some reason it had never even occurred to me that this was going to be a drinking party. My geeky, freshman self assumed that Lauren's parents would be home and that everyone would just be hanging out after the game. That was nothing like what I actually saw.

There were kids everywhere. The living room, dining room and kitchen were packed. I instantly started to get nervous and tried to grab Gia and back down the hallway to get some space. Instead I bumped into two seniors who were making out. The guy had his hand up her shirt, and she held a beer with one hand and was running her hand through his hair with the other. I jumped back, mortified that I had bumped into them, but they didn't even stop for a second. I noticed that two or three other couples were doing the exact same thing all down the hall. The thought of what must be going on in the bedrooms made my stomach flip flop.

Music was blaring, and kids had set up drinking games everywhere. Some were flipping cups over on a table, then chugging their beers, and others were shooting little ping pong balls into lined up cups and drinking. Gia and I glanced at each other, and I could tell she was just as uncomfortable as me.

"Let's try and go outside," she said and grabbed my hand to lead me out back. We stepped out onto the patio, hoping for a breath of air and some time to think. Instead we found Kelly, the other cheerleaders, and half the football players sitting around a fire in the chimea, next to the covered pool. I rushed over to my sister.

"Kell, this is crazy," I whispered in her ear. "We have to leave. Dad would kill us if he knew we were at a drinking party."

"What did you think it was gonna be, Kate?" she acted as if it was the most normal thing in the world that we were at a party with a bunch of underage, drunk kids. We had never done anything like this before.

"Kelly, you're nuts," I begged her, "seriously, we are going to get in so much trouble. There's no way we won't get caught."

"Look, I'm happy we got invited. I'm not drinking, you're not drinking, so who cares if other people are? Stop being such a spaz, Kate. Maybe it would be good for you to loosen up and have some fun."

Kelly walked away from me, so that there was no way I could continue the conversation. Gia slowly walked over.

"It doesn't look like that went well," she said gently. "What do you want to do? Stay? Leave? It's up to you."

"I don't know," I stammered, "What do you think?"

"Kate, you know this isn't my kind of thing," Gia said, "But you also know my parents could care less where I am right now, so I'm not going to get in trouble. If you need me to stay with you, I will. That's what friends are for."

At least I always knew I could count on Gopi and Gia. If only my sister could be as supportive as them.

"Let's stay for an hour, try to find Jada again, make sure Kelly doesn't do anything stupid, and find Jake. Then I really do want to get out of here. I'm going to feel horrible lying to my dad."

I glanced over one last time at Kelly, hoping she would come to her senses and walk back over to me and Gia, but she was laughing with some other girls, and perching on the lap of some junior football player. At least she had kept her word about drinking and there wasn't a beer in her hand.

We walked back into the house just in time to see a girl stand up, start to try and walk towards the back door, and then throw up five feet from where we were standing.

"Ew!" Gia screamed jumping backwards and almost knocking me over.

"Lauren!" a few girls yelled, "Come quick we gotta clean this up!"

The girl who had thrown up, slumped down against a wall and seemed to fall asleep.

"Should we see if she's OK?" I asked Gia.

"It's not our problem, and I don't want to get puked on," she said, "Come on, let's find Jada."

We headed back towards the living room. There were kids watching a Flyers game on TV, kids still playing the drinking games, girls dancing on the stairs, and the couples still gung-ho making out in the hallway, but no Jada. I noticed that some of the girls who were dancing were from the soccer team, but I was too shy to ask them if they'd seen her.

"Do you think she's upstairs?" I asked Gia.

"I don't know, I'll ask the girls we came with if they've seen her. Where's your boyfriend? Shouldn't he have found you by now?"

"He must not be here yet, or he would have," I assured her.

Gia was apparently much less shy than me, and she walked right up to the dancing girls to ask where Jada was. Then she came back over and started pulling me towards the hallway again.

"Where are we going?"

"Apparently there's a rec room downstairs that more people are in. They think Jada must be there," Gia said as she maneuvered past the couples groping each other.

We found the stairs and headed down into a big, open refinished basement. There was a pool table in front of us with a bunch of kids around it, to the side there were couches filled with kids smoking, and then a group of kids playing Wii on a big TV set. We scanned the corners for Jada, and then headed towards the couches to try and find her.

I scanned the faces of the kids, and was shocked to see Jake.

"Jake!" I yelled, rushing over to sit by him. The girl next to him didn't move an inch, and Jake rolled his head towards me, but didn't get up.

"Heeeeyyyyyyyy, Katie," he said and started to laugh uncontrollably.

"Jake, where were you? I thought you weren't here yet. Why didn't you find me?" I squeezed in next to him on the couch, ignoring the girl's glare.

"Uh-oh! Jakey boy's got trouble with his little freshman girlie!" One of the senior football players yelled out, and the rest of them started cracking up hysterically.

My face flushed its usual shade of bright red, and my hands started shaking. The last thing I needed was to come off as some crazy, psycho girlfriend, but I couldn't understand why Jake hadn't found me. It wasn't like him. I looked over to see his response and noticed that his eyes were shut and he was lying back down on the side of the couch.

"Jake," I whispered, "what's wrong? Are you sick?"

Gia leaned over the back of the couch, "He's not sick, Kate, he's drunk. Come on let's get out of here."

I was stunned. How could Jake do this? He had never drank before! Mrs. Williams was going to kill him. What if he got grounded and we couldn't go to homecoming? How could he have sat and drank with these stupid football players and never even came and found me?

"Jake," I whispered loudly in his ear, "are you drunk?!"

His eyes half opened and he gave that goofy chuckle again, "Chill out, Kates, I had like three beers. Don't worry, I still love you."

I looked at Jake with disgust and got up to head towards Gia.

"How could he do this? This isn't like him at all!" I said to her as we hurried to get away.

"Kate, don't be too mad at him. He probably has a lot of pressure from the older guys on the team to party with them. It's kinda normal. He shouldn't have done it, but it was just once, and you know how good he is to you. Talk to him tomorrow, but give him another chance," Gia said.

She was probably right. I knew Jake was under a lot of pressure to seem cool to the older guys on the team. Still though, I didn't approve of drinking at all. He was going to have to promise me that this would never happen again.

And if he got caught tonight, I thought he kind of deserved it.

We made our way down the make-out hallway one last time.

"I have no idea where Jada is," Gia said.

"Let me make sure Kelly's OK, and then let's get out of here," I said. "I guess we'll find out what happened to Jada tomorrow."

We walked across the kitchen trying not to step where the girl had thrown up. Someone had wiped it up with paper towels but the floor was still disgustingly sticky. I tried to tell myself that it was from all the spilled beer and not the vomit, so that I wouldn't start to feel queasy.

When we stepped onto the patio, I saw that Kell had kept her word and still wasn't drinking. She sat in a chair just laughing and watching the kids goofing off. When she saw me come out, she jumped up and hurried over.

"I'm sorry Kate, I know you don't like these kind of things. I should have been more understanding, it's just that I was having a really good time and I didn't want it to be ruined," Kelly said softly.

I stared at her, unsure of whether I was ready to forgive her or not.

"Please don't tell Dad," she pleaded with me, "I promise I won't come to anything like this again until we're much older. You're right; we really could get in a lot of trouble."

"If you come with us now, I won't tell Dad," I said, "but honestly, Kelly, you have to promise to stay away from things like this again. It would kill him if he knew we were at a party like this."

"OK I'll come," she agreed, "Let me just say goodbye."

"Thank God," Gia said, "Let's get out of here. I'm gonna call my mom and tell her to pick us up in half an hour at the McDonalds on Route 47, so we're gonna have to walk over to it. It's like ten minutes away."

Kelly walked around hugging all of her cheerleader friends and flirtatiously saying goodbye to the boy she'd been hanging around. It was probably the guy that she'd been texting lately. I decided it wasn't worth my time to say goodbye to Jake. I figured Trey would get him home. We walked around the side of the house to leave, instead of having to go back inside. As we picked our way around the bushes, we heard someone. There was a girl sitting by herself on the edge of the porch, making soft gasping sounds that were unmistakably someone who was crying and trying not to be heard. As we got closer to the person, we realized who it was.

"Jada?" Gia exclaimed. "Oh my God, are you alright?"

She lifted her head and we could see the tears on her face, the swollen eyes, and her smeared makeup.

"What happened?" Kelly said, sitting down to rub her back.

Jada turned her face to the side, and rubbed at her eyes again.

"Were you drinking?" Gia asked, "Are you sick?"

Jada shook her head, and tears welled up fresh in her eyes again.

"You can tell us," I said gently, "It's alright."

"Let's just get out of here," were the first words out of Jada's mouth. "Do you guys have a way to get home?'

"We're gonna walk to McDonalds, then my mom is picking us up. She won't ask any questions about where we've been," Gia said.

"OK let's go," Jada said getting up and rubbing at her eyes a final time.

On the walk to McDonalds Jada told us what had happened. All week Trey had been texting her, writing to her on Facebook, and he had even called her about coming to this party. She had been really excited because she had such a crush on him.

"It was like the first guy I've ever really liked, you know?" she said in hurt voice.

I realized that it was probably the first guy who had ever hurt her, too.

"Well, what happened?" Kelly asked, "Did he ignore you?"

"No," Jada explained, "It was much worse."

She went on to tell us how Trey had found her the second we got to the party, when she first split up from me and Gia. He'd asked her to be his beer pong partner (I figured that was the game they'd been playing) and gotten her to drink some. When Jada didn't want to drink anymore, Trey had suggested they go upstairs, and he took her up to a room and started kissing her.

"At first it was so awesome," she said tearing up again, "I thought he really liked me, but then when I wouldn't let him get past second base, he started to get really mean. He told me he shouldn't have wasted his time on an immature freshman."

"What a jerk!" I said, "I can't believe that its Jake's brother you're talking about!"

"It gets worse," she continued, "After he said that, we got up to leave, and he didn't say one word to me. When we walked out in the hallway, a senior girl I don't even know came up to him all flirtatiously and asked what he was doing hanging out with a little freshman. Then he just looked at me, said he didn't know, and turned and went back in the room with her!"

"He's an asshole," Gia said, rubbing her back, "You don't need him."

"I know," Jada said, "It's just that I really thought he liked me. I feel so stupid."

"If it makes you feel any better Jake was a jerk tonight too," I offered, "he got drunk and totally ignored me."

"Maybe this should show us something guys," Gia said, "Friends should be more important than guys. We're all drifting apart a little since we started school, and you guys know that. Let's try to forget about all the stupid drama at Adam's Prep, and focus on what's important – each other."

I knew that what Gia said was right, and I desperately wanted to believe her. But as we climbed into her mom's car and I looked at the faces of my sister and my best friends, I knew that as positive as I had been trying to be, as much as I'd tried to ignore it, and as much as I loved them, things were a little different. I just hoped that we could all listen to Gia and get back to how we used to be.

## Chapter 11

"Umm, it's a little much," I said cringing at the short, tight, leopard print dress Jada was trying on for homecoming.

""Your're out of your mind," Gopi said shaking her head. "It breaks like every Adam's dress code there is."

"Your Dad's the one whose gonna lose his mind if you try and go out in that," Kelly piped in.

"Alright, alright I get the point," Jada said, stomping back into the changing room. "It's just that if I have to go to this dance alone, I at least wanted to look fabulous."

"You're not the only one going alone," I comforted her, "Gia's going stag, too."

"And I'm not even going!" Gopi said in an annoyed voice, "and to make matters worse, my parents scheduled my first night of SAT tutoring for Friday. I'm not even taking the SAT for *two years*! Everybody else is going to be at the Homecoming Dance, and I'm going to be doing analogies."

"We'll miss you though, Gopi," Gia said smiling, "Plus it's not really even that big of a deal, it's just a school dance. I actually do have a date though, guys."

"What?!" Kelly exclaimed, "You didn't even tell us! Who is he?"

"His name is John, and he's a junior in my Art class. He's pretty cool. He's from Haddon Township and just transferred to Adam's this year, so he doesn't have many friends. We actually talk a lot," Gia said.

"You never even told us!" Jada said, popping back out of the changing room.

"You never asked," Gia shrugged, "You've kind of been in your own world of the soccer girls, and Trey up until this Friday."

Jada's face dropped at the mention of Trey's name.

"I'm sorry, Jada, I didn't mean to bring that up and upset you," Gia said.

"No it's cool," Jada said, "He was a jerk. I'm just glad I know now to be more careful. Plus it's helped me realize again who my real friends are. Would you believe that now Madison is talking to Trey even though I told her what he did to me?!"

"Believe it? Yeah, she's a bitch. I hope she gets what she deserves," I said.

"Wow, Kate, you never talk like that!" said Kelly.

"She's right," Gopi said, "She's horrid. I still can't believe what she said about my father. I think those two are a perfect match."

Gia interrupted our gossip, "Oh this is the perfect one!" She twirled around to show us all the dress. It was black, of course, but it had tons of little rhinestones dotting the top, and a cute, bright pink sash that tied in a side bow. It was adorable, and it fit her perfectly.

"I love it!" I said.

"Me too!" said Kelly.

Gopi and Jada chimed in that they loved it too.

"Well, now the twins and I have our dresses," Gia said, "Jada, did you find anything?"

"I might just wear the turquoise one I wore to graduation," Jada replied, "or come back with my mom. I just can't find anything today."

"Let's go eat then," Gopi said, "I'm starving, and at least if I'm not allowed to pick out dresses and go to dances, I can still eat ice cream."

As we headed towards the food court I started thinking about the dance. My dress was perfect; short, black, kind of tight, and very un-Katie like. It was exactly what I needed. Miss Linda had already taken me and Kelly shopping. Kell had picked out a bright, pink dress. She was going with a sophomore who played football, named Andrew. It was weird, she never really talked about him, but she must really like him because the whispered calls and secret texts had almost doubled. I still couldn't figure out why she wasn't talking to me about him though.

After the incident with Trey, Jada had decided that all boys were idiots and she was just going to go to the Homecoming herself. That way, she could relax and have fun. And apparently now Gia had a date too. Everything should have been perfect, but something was still a little off, and I knew exactly what it was.

Jake and I had pretty much made up for the other night. I took Gia's advice and tried to understand that there must be a lot of pressure on him from the older boys on the team, but I also made him swear that he would never drink again, or act like a complete jerk like his brother had. But despite him swearing up and down that he would never be like Trey, that he had made a huge mistake, and that he loved me, we weren't as close as usual. The party had definitely made things a little awkward between us. Hopefully the Homecoming Dance would be a perfect night and we could get back to being like we were for the past year and two months.

**Chapter 12**

I walked quickly towards my seat as the bell rang for homeroom. Immediately everyone got quiet as the intro music played and our school's news crew came on with the morning announcements. I stared up at the screen and doodled on my handbook while they read the daily school and sports updates.

"Homeroom Reps, I need you to come here for a second," Mr. Sewell said.

My stomach plummeted. I had almost forgotten about the first day of school when I found out I had to be a Homeroom Representative because nothing had ever been said about it since then. My head started to fill with all the horrible thoughts of things I might find out I had to do. I slowly stood up and moped back to Mr. Sewell's desk.

"I'm not sure if you guys know this," Mr. Sewell began, "but the Homeroom Reps have to represent the freshman level in all school sponsored contests and activities. Therefore at the Homecoming Dance you two will have to participate in the dance contest against the other grade levels."

"Awesome!" Marcus said. "I'll get to show my moves."

I couldn't even speak. A dance contest? In front of the entire school? I had failed 4-year-old ballerina class because I was so uncoordinated, and now I was going to have to be in a dance contest? In front of everyone at the Homecoming Dance? I didn't think I could have come up with a worse scenario for what the Homeroom Reps had to do, if I'd tried.

"I, um, I….I'm not really a good dancer," I stammered. I was desperate to come up with an excuse to get out of this.

"Ah, don't worry about it," Mr. Sewell laughed. "The contests are rigged anyway, so that the seniors always win. You would still come in last place even if you were a good dancer because the freshmen always lose. It's an Adam's tradition; you'll like it a lot better when you're a senior."

He picked up a stack of papers and started grading them, as if nothing had just happened. I stood still for a minute, unsure of whether the conversation was really just going to end on that note. Was I supposed to feel some sort of consolation from what he said?

"No way, Mr. Sewell," Marcus said, "my moves are so good, there's no way some senior can beat me."

Mr.Sewell laughed, but in a nice way, "Well, Marcus, I wish you luck. I'd love to see the seniors lose for once, but it's going to be a tough battle for you, since the contest is judged by the members of the Senior Board."

"Just wait, Mr. Sewell," Marcus said smiling from ear to ear, "I'll charm 'em. You'll see. Me and Katie are gonna be hot."

Hot was definitely one word to describe how I was feeling. Not in any form of the context that Marcus was referring to, but if my cheeks burned any redder, I thought they might actually catch on fire. Really, a dance contest? With me as one of the people representing the freshman class? I was the type of girl to represent the freshmen class in an essay contest, a spelling bee, a school-wide pop quiz – but a dance contest? My perfect homecoming night suddenly didn't seem so perfect anymore.

## Chapter 13

I flopped onto Kelly's bed and rolled over onto my back.

"I'm not going to Homecoming anymore," I said and started playing with a stuffed frog that was lying next to her pillow.

Kelly's head quickly snapped away from the computer.

"WHAT?!!" she said in a shocked voice, "I thought for once you were excited instead of nervous. This is a big dance, Kate."

"I was excited, until today."

Kelly squinched her face up like she'd just tasted something sour, then quickly looked back at the computer.

"What happened?" she asked, "Did you and Jake get in a fight?"

"No its worse," I whined. "You know how I got picked for the stupid Homeroom Rep thing? Well, all the Homeroom Reps have to compete in a dance contest representing our level at Homecoming!"

"So," Kelly shrugged without taking her eyes away from the computer screen.

"SOOOOOOOOOOOOOOO, it's like my worst nightmare: getting up in front of everyone and dancing. I'll probably fall and make an idiot out of myself," I said.

"I think it sounds like fun," Kelly said. "It's really not that big of deal. I think you're overreacting a little."

For whatever reason, my sister was not giving me any sympathy. Usually I could come to her with my feelings and problems. She was the only person who really understood me. She was who I'd turned to my whole life. Why was she acting like this didn't matter at all?

"Kelly, why are you blowing me off? You know what things are like for me, how nervous I get. In fact you're the *only* one who knows. Ever since mom left, you're who I've talked to."

"Oh great, here we go again with mom!" Kelly said with exasperation in her voice, "Mom left when we were three. We're about to turn fifteen, do you think at any point you might get over it, Kate?"

"Whatever! Forget I even said anything!" I yelled, jumping up to storm out of her room.

"Katie, stop," Kelly said grabbing my sleeve. "You're right; I guess I'm being too harsh. It just doesn't seem like that big of a deal to me. I guess for once I just wanted to go to an event, besides a sleepover with our friends, where I knew you were gonna just relax and we could all have fun."

I thought over what Kelly had just said for minute. Maybe she was right. I mean I hated how I always got panicky, why wouldn't she hate it too? It had never occurred to me how my nervousness might make my sister feel.

"I guess I never thought of it that way," I said. "I'm sorry. I'll try to chill out a little so we can have more fun at things."

"And I'll try not to say anything mean again," Kelly said softly. "I know how things are for you. It's just that sometimes I think we're really different."

I walked back over, sat on the bed, picked the frog up and started tugging at his soft, pink little tongue. I wanted to go back to when we both loved Disney princesses, red fruit snacks and Candy Land, I didn't want to be growing up into two different people. But as usual, Kelly was OK with everything, and I felt like the one left behind.

"Hey, I actually have an idea!" she said. "How well does Mr. Sewell know you?"

"Not really at all. I just have him for homeroom," I said.

"Perfect! Then he'll never know the difference!" Kelly replied. "I'll do the dance contest for you. I love to dance, and I think we still look enough alike that none of the teachers will even notice."

"You will?" I said rushing over to hug my sister, who suddenly seemed not quite so distant anymore.

"Yep, it's settled. Now we can relax, get through the next two days, and have an awesome time on Friday."

"That sounds perfect!" I said as a wave of relief rushed over me.

Just then Kelly's phone started ringing.

"Um, I'm gonna take this. It's someone from cheerleading. Do you mind giving me some privacy?" she asked.

"Not a problem," I replied and headed to my room. I started my homework so that I could get everything done and just relax and have fun this weekend. I could do that, relax a little. Maybe Kelly was right, maybe I gave into my feelings too much. Maybe it was time for me to start making some changes. It certainly seemed like everything else in my life had been changing, regardless of whether I liked it or not.

## Chapter 14

When I looked in the mirror I hardly recognized the girl looking back at me. My dress was not my usual style. It was short, tight and black and it looked amazing. My hair was pulled half back with two sparkly, silver barrettes and curled. My makeup was done perfectly. I was wearing my new necklace from Jake and diamond earrings. The memory of the moment he gave it to me made me blush all over again, and I smiled at the pretty girl in the mirror. It was hard to believe it was me.

Kelly was already downstairs when I heard the doorbell ring.

"Katie, I think Jake's here. Hurry down, Sweetie!" Dad yelled up.

I glanced one last time in the mirror to make sure everything was perfect. Then I reached down and picked up the picture of my mother.

"It's an important night, Mom." I whispered softly. "Another important night and you're missing it again." Part of me desperately wanted everything that happened in the past eleven years to disappear and for me to walk downstairs and she'd be there, waiting to take our picture and hug us goodbye. The other part of me wanted what Kelly had said the other night to come true; that I would stop being the girl upstairs whispering to pictures and be able to just rush downstairs and enjoy a perfect night with my friends.

"You know what, Mom," I set the picture down as I was talking, "This time I'm gonna be the one to walk away." I set down the picture, looked up at the mirror and smiled at my reflection. Then I rushed downstairs to enjoy my night.

"Let me get one more of the whole group," Dad said, lining up Jake and I, Kelly and Andrew, Gia and John, and Jada.

He snapped another picture, and so did the other parents.

"It's a shame Gopi will miss this," Jada's mom said.

"I have an idea!" Jada said, "Take one of all of us with my phone and I'll text it to her, to tell her we miss her."

"Good idea!" I exclaimed. We took one more, and sent it to her with four identical texts.

*Wish you were here! We luv u!!!!!!*

She immediately texted us all back, saying that she was fine and she hoped we would have fun. Gopi was a great friend. I was really going to miss her tonight.

"Are you ready?" Jake asked as he put is his arm around my waist.

I smiled. I realized it was actually the first thing he'd said to me tonight. Maybe all the pictures were making him nervous.

"Just one sec," I replied. I walked over and gave Dad a kiss goodbye. "Thank you," I said and kissed him on the cheek.

"For what?"

"For being a good dad," I replied. I think he understood that I actually meant a whole lot more than that. Then I walked over to Miss Linda and gave her the first hug I had ever given her. "Thanks for coming, Miss Linda. It was really nice of you to spend your Friday night doing this."

"No problem, Katie," she smiled. "I hope you guys all have fun."

"I hope you two do, too!" I said in a sing song voice, as I ran out the door and climbed into the back of Mrs. Brown's minivan, right next to Jake, who was next to Kelly and Andrew.

"It's a tight squeeze everyone," Mrs. Brown said. "Make sure you buckle up."

"You guys smell the same," Jake laughed, leaning back and forth from me to my sister.

"That's because I always sneak and use Katie's perfume," Kelly smiled.

I smiled back. I didn't mind at all if we smelled the same. Nothing could ruin this night.

After I fastened my seat belt, Jake leaned over and took my hand. "You look really pretty tonight," he said.

"Thanks," I replied. "You look nice too."

"Ugh," Jada groaned under her breath, "How can Jake be so sweet and his brother be such a jerk?"

"Sorry about that, Jada," Jake blushed. "Let's just forget that whole party. None of us should have gone. Can we just try and have fun tonight?"

"Definitely," Jada said with a smile.

"Yep, this is gonna be the best night ever," I added.

"I agree," Kelly chimed in.

"Me too," said Gia.

Finally we were there. The gym at Adam's Prep looked nothing like it ever had before. The entire room was dark, except for the flashing, colored lights on the dance floor. The floor felt like it was moving from the vibrations of the loud music. Maroon and silver streamers and balloons seemed to cover every inch of the walls and ceiling, and the entire gym was packed with kids.

We handed the chaperone our tickets, and walked towards the bleachers to lay our coats down. Somehow, out of the 800 kids packed into that gym, Madison DiCicco managed to find us first.

"Hey girls!" she screamed and ran up to Jada and Kelly to hug them. "Hiiii, Jake!"

She acted as if Gia and I weren't even alive. Ugh!

"Do you guys wanna dance?" she asked jumping up and down.

"Let's go!" Jada agreed.

"I'll hang here with Jake," I said.

"Actually, Kate, do you mind going with them?" Jake asked. "I gotta find the guys from the team, and then I'll come get you."

"Um, I guess," I said. Of course I minded. The last person I wanted to hang out with tonight was Madison; plus I was kinda hurt that Jake was disappearing on me.

Kelly grabbed my hand and pulled me out to the dance floor with Jada and Madison. Gia hung back with John to get a drink. There had to be about thirty girls from our freshman class all dancing in a pack together. The music was loud and people were grinding and dancing kind of crazy. I couldn't believe I was stuck dancing with Madison, but I tried to push the thought out of my mind. At first I was nervous, and then I realized there were so many people on the dance floor that there was no way anyone was going to notice me in particular. I actually started to relax and have fun. Two songs in, Gia and John joined us. I was having fun dancing with my friends, but I kept wondering where Jake was. After about four songs, a slow one came on. I looked around for Jake, but didn't see him anywhere. I started to follow Jada off the dance floor, when I felt a hand on my back.

"Where you going, Kates?" Jake said smiling, "I was just coming to find you. This is perfect timing."

As usual, my heart melted. Jake wrapped his arms around me, and I laid my head on his shoulder. It felt so nice and familiar with my face against him; the smell of his cologne, the softness of his cheek, the tiny freckles that only I had ever seen up close, they all reminded me of how much I loved him. I wished the song would never end, but all too soon the floor started bouncing again and hundreds of kids came rushing back out, as yet another hip hop song started to play.

Jada and Gia came back out to join us. The four of us danced for a few more songs, and then Jake and I decided to get a drink.

"I wonder where Kelly is?" I said as Jake handed me a Coke.

Jake just shrugged, "How would I know? Hey, I gotta find the guys again. Meet you in a bit, OK?" Jake rushed off before I even had a chance to answer. Why did he keep doing this? Were the football guys that important that he couldn't focus on me for one night? I started to get annoyed again. Then I realized that I was standing alone, so I quickly headed back over to where my friends were. They had decided to take a break too and were sitting on the bleachers. Thankfully, Madison had finally left. I plopped next to Jada because Gia was next to her date.

"Have you guys seen Kelly?" I asked.

"No, I figured she was with her new man," Jada shrugged. "Who is he anyway? She's, like, barely talked about him."

"I don't know," I said, "but I think she really likes him because she's constantly texting him and talking to him on the computer. I have no idea why it's so secretive though."

"Maybe she just really likes him," Gia piped in. "I don't think Kelly's ever really liked someone before. It could be making her act differently. Speaking of people you two really like, where's Jake? We've barely seen him tonight."

"I know," I said. "And it's starting to piss me off. When I do see him, the nights perfect, so why does he keep disappearing?"

"You don't think he's drinking again, do you?" Jada said raising her eyebrows. "I heard that some of the football players were sneaking out to their cars to drink."

I thought it over for a minute, and I started to get a little mad. He had promised he wouldn't drink again, and this was supposed to be our night. Plus my dad and Miss Linda were picking us up. Jake absolutely could not show up drunk in front of my father.

"I have to find him," I said, "I'm gonna kill him if he is. I'll meet you guys back here in a little bit, don't move OK?"

I got up and made my way through the gym towards the door. I decided it wasn't worth putting my coat on, since I had every intention of making Jake come right back inside. I walked out the main door and started to scan the parking lot. Sure enough in the back corner where it was darker, I saw a bunch of figures huddled around some cars. I decided my best bet was to quietly walk up, and back away quickly if he wasn't there, or discreetly grab him if he was. The last thing I wanted was to make a scene. It would be humiliating if I did.

I walked softly towards the cars, thinking about the least embarrassing way to approach this. Suddenly I noticed two people leaning against the car right in front of me kissing. In an instant I saw the short blonde hair, his blue shirt, the unmistakable look of his hands and fingernails that I had memorized over the last year of our relationship.

Jake was kissing another girl.

In the same instant, that I realized what was happening I saw her long blonde hair.

Madison!

It was all happening so quickly, I didn't even know what I was doing. Instinct and anger made me rush over. I was about five feet away from pulling Madison off of him and punching her in the face, when something caught my attention. She was wearing a bright pink dress.

"Oh my God," was all that I managed to mumble, as I stumbled backwards from the shock.

It was Kelly. My sister. My twin sister. And she had her tongue down my boyfriend's throat and his hands were all over her. For a second the unbelievable shock froze me right where I was. It wasn't Madison, the girl that I'd thought was my worst enemy. It was Kelly, who I'd thought was my best friend.

Somehow a mixture of anger, numbness, and sharp pain all seemed to hit me at once. My legs felt weak, my chest hurt, and my fists clenched. Before I even knew what I was doing, I heard myself say in a short, harsh voice, "Does she just smell like me, Jake, or does she kiss like me too?"

As soon as they heard my voice, both of them jumped back, shocked.

"Kate!" Kelly said instantly moving away from Jake, "Wait!"

My entire body went numb then. It was like every time I had ever been embarrassed or nervous times a thousand. The world seemed to stand still as Kelly looked pleadingly at me and Jake stared at the ground. I wanted to scream. I wanted to tell them both how much I hated them. I wanted to make them feel one ounce of the pain that they had just caused me. I wanted them to know how hurt, how betrayed, I was. But when I looked at my sister, no words would come out of my mouth. I unclenched my fists, realizing there was no way I was going to actually hit anyone.

I started stumbling backwards, thinking I might throw up. A wave of heat rushed over me.

"Katie, please," Kelly said running towards me, "I'm sorry. It just happened. Neither of us meant for it to. We couldn't help it."

She reached where I was standing, and wrapped her arms around me. I turned and looked at her and a feeling of anger like I had never felt before came over me. I pushed her arms off and shoved her away. She had no right to hug me right now.

"Kates!" Jake yelled, but I had finally gotten my legs to start moving again and I ran back in the gym.

The lights seemed to swirl around me, and the pulsating music was an overload.

There were so many people.

It was so loud.

Kelly had just kissed Jake.

I found a wall, and leaned back against it, then slumped down to the ground because I started to feel faint. It was odd though, for whatever reason, I didn't cry. I think I was too shocked to even cry.

Gia found me first. "Katie, there you are!" she said rushing over. "We've been looking for you everywhere! You never came back to meet us."

I looked up at her, and she instantly knew something was wrong.

"Oh my God, Katie, what happened? Was he drinking again?"

At first I couldn't even find the words to tell her what had happened. I felt like if I said it, then it would really be real.

"Is that it, Kate?" Gia asked again.

"Do you want me to go out there?" John offered.

I looked up at my friend's face and forced myself to admit that it was real. I had to tell her.

"I just saw Jake and Kelly making out," I managed to mutter. Just saying it made it hurt all over again.

The look of shock on Gia's face was genuine. At least I knew then that I wasn't the only one who hadn't known.

"Oh Katie, are you OK?" She sat down next to me and wrapped her arms around me. Just then Kelly came up behind us. At least she had, had the sense not to bring Jake.

"Katie," she started, but the looks that Gia and I gave her were enough to get her to shut up.

As if by some cruel twist of fate, right then Mr. Summers came on the microphone asking for all students participating in the dance contest to come to stage.

"I'll go for you, Kate," Kelly said softly.

"No," I said in the most assertive tone I had ever used in my life.

I stood up and looked my sister right in the eye. Kelly looked stunned, and that helped to increase my determination."I can take care of myself," I said.

I was determined to never need her help again. I swallowed, took a deep breath and marched up to the stage. I found my place next to Marcus and stared out at the bright lights. I didn't even feel nervous, just numb. I felt like I was watching a movie of all this happening, rather than it really happening to me.

When Mr. Summers called our names, Marcus took my hand. "You ready?" he asked.

I figured there was absolutely no way that the night could possibly get any worse, so I nodded and followed him out. When the song started playing, we danced along with the twenty-something other Homeroom Reps that were freshmen. I focused on the beat, put a smile on my face, and followed Marcus' lead. The music blared, the lights were shining hotly on us, and the faces of the cheering crowd were a blur. At one point I knew I saw Jada cheering us on, and a few familiar faces flashed by as I twisted and turned, but there was no sign of Jake or Kelly. Before I knew it, it was over.

I had actually competed in the dance contest, and I had done just fine.

"Nice job!" Marcus said smiling.

"Thanks," I managed a smile back, "you too."

"I hope we win, though!" he said emphatically.

"In a weird way, I kinda already did," I said, much more for my own benefit than Marcus'. I ignored the puzzled look on his face and headed off the dance floor.

Gia rushed over and handed me my coat. "I called my mom. She's on her way and we'll get you home."

"I don't want to ruin your night too," I said.

"It's nothing, Katie, John and I can hang out at my house. You know I don't really like these things anyway. I just want to make sure you're OK," she replied.

I was really grateful to her at that moment. Absolutely nothing sounded better than going home. For a second, out of habit, I started to worry about how Kelly would get home. Then I immediately stopped myself. She and Jake could figure out their own way home – they deserved each other.

"Thank you, Gia," I mumbled, letting her lead me out. "I'm not OK, though."

"I know," she said rubbing my back, "and wish I knew what to say to make it better."

On the ride home the tears finally started to come. They ran like hot streams down the side of my face, and by the time I got to my house my makeup was smeared, my face was red, and my eyes were swollen. I desperately just wanted to crawl into bed.

Gia followed me out of the car and asked her mom to wait for a minute.

"I'll explain what happened to your dad, so you don't have to," she said.

I just nodded. We walked in the door and I headed straight for the stairs, as Gia walked towards the living room to find my dad. When I got to my room, I grabbed the picture of my mom off of my desk and climbed into bed without even bothering to take my dress off. I leaned back against the pillows, hugged the picture to my chest and let myself cry.

A few minutes later there was a gentle knock on the door.

"Katie," Dad said, "Are you OK?"

He slowly opened the door and walked over to sit at the edge of my bed.

"I still love her too, you know," he said.

I rolled my eyes. This was not what I wanted to hear.

"I know you still love her Dad, she's your daughter. But what she did to me tonight was horrible!" I said.

Dad smiled gently, "That's not what I meant, Sweetie. Of course I still love Kelly, although rest assured she will be in quite a bit of trouble for treating you like this." He continued, "I meant I still love your mother."

I looked up, stunned at what he had said. I had forgotten that I was holding the picture when he came in.

"But," I stammered, "you never talk about her. How can you love her?"

"I can't talk about her," he said. "She hurt me too badly and it still upsets me. But don't think that a day goes by when I don't think about her."

"I know she hurt you, Dad, but she couldn't have hurt you as badly as I was hurt tonight."

"You'd be surprised, Kates, we were married. Being betrayed by your wife is kind of worse than being betrayed by your high school boyfriend."

"Yeah," I said, "but she didn't leave you for Uncle Steve! Jake did this to me with my own sister!"

Dad lay back next to me and put his arms around me.

"No, Sweetie, she didn't," he said softly stroking my hair, "but she also hurt my little girls, and there is no one in the world that I love more than them."

I curled up onto his chest and let myself cry there for a minute.

"I'm sorry, Katie," Dad whispered.

"It's not your fault," I said. "It's Kelly and Jake's."

"No, I'm sorry for never talking to you about your mother," he said. "I'm sorry for letting you think you were the only one who still missed her."

He kissed my forehead, "and I'm sorry for what you went through tonight."

"Thanks, Dad," I said. I gave him one last hug.

"Can I just go to sleep now?" I asked.

Dad nodded and quietly got up. I sank down into my pillows, under the covers and let the soft warmth of them comfort me. I started quietly crying again, thinking about what I had seen and the impact it would have on my life. Then I slowly cried myself to sleep.

## Chapter 15

The sun shining on my face woke me up the next morning. I rolled over and sunk back down into my soft blankets. The itch on my back made me realize that I was still wearing my dress from the night before. Then the events from last night came rushing back to me all at once. I kept seeing the image of Kelly and Jake kissing over and over in my head. My eyes started to swell up with tears all over again. I decided I needed to go down to the lake to think.

I got out of bed and put on some comfy sweats. I grabbed my backpack and shoved two blankets in it, one to lie on, and one in case it was too cold. Then I reached under my pillow, grabbed the birthday card and shoved it in my bag. I made sure to be quiet as I went down the hall because the last thing I wanted right now was to see my sister.

In the kitchen, I grabbed a bottle of water, and considered taking a package of Pop-Tarts. Then I decided that there was no way I was going to be able to eat, so I headed out the back door and into the yard.

The blueberry bushes were nothing but twigs now, and the roses were all gone. I lifted the latch to the gate, and headed down towards the lake. It was early in the morning and although it was October, the sun was shining so it wasn't too cold. Like I had many times before, I laid down on my blanket to think.

My head started swirling with a million thoughts. I felt like I was in overload. I needed to sort things out, to calm down a little, but it didn't seem like that was going to happen.

Over and over the scenes from last night played in my head: Jake disappearing, Kelly disappearing too, how close I'd felt to him when we were dancing, thinking he was drinking again. Then, worst of all, the image that was forever burned into my head, of my sister and Jake kissing.

Suddenly it occurred to me that it hadn't all just happened that night. The texts, the phone calls, the computer conversations, there was never some mystery guy. My sister had been talking to my boyfriend all along and I was too stupid to have any idea. Anger welled up in me just as it did last night. How long had this been going on? Worse yet, how long would they have continued it if I hadn't found them?

Thoughts continued to rush through my head. I felt so many emotions at once: shock, anger, jealousy, embarrassment. And then the same question over and over -*How could I really have had no idea?*

Eventually, I realized why I had no idea – because it was never something I would have done. In a million years, I wouldn't have hurt my sister like she hurt me. I had truly felt she was my best friend. The one person I needed most in this world, had betrayed me.

Worse yet, I knew I hated Jake now. I knew he had hurt me terribly and I never wanted to see him again, but I also knew that it didn't even compare to how hurt I felt by Kelly.

I leaned back against my backpack, overwhelmed with my own thoughts. I let the sun shine on my face and tried to think straight, so that I could calm down. I started taking deep breaths in and clearing my head. My phone beeped over and over. Finally, I glanced at it. I had texts from Gia, Gopi and Jada; they all knew what happened by now. They just wanted to make sure I was OK, and I appreciated it, but I couldn't answer them right now. I needed to just lie still.

Then I heard the footsteps approaching from about a hundred feet away and instantly knew whose they were.

"Katie," Kelly said in a gentle tone, "I'm so sorry! I can't ..."

I cut her off. "Not now, Kelly. I really can't even listen to you right now," I said.

Again I saw the image of her and Jake in my head. I thought of all the lies she'd told me in the past few weeks since we started high school. These were the weeks when I'd needed her the most. I got so angry that I couldn't even look at her.

She stood awkwardly at the edge of my blanket, but I just stared straight ahead at the lake. Silence surrounded us. Out of anger, my first real conclusion from the whole situation suddenly came to me.

"You know what, Kell," I said in a bitter tone, "at least I figured out why it was so easy for you to just let Mom go. Why all of those nights that I missed her, and all those times that I tried to talk to you about her, you could just shrug it off. I finally figured out what kind of little girl could just forget about her mother."

"What? Why?" Kelly asked in astonishment.

"The kind who's just like her," I said through my teeth. "That's what you are. You're just like mom. You can turn your back on the people that love you the most."

Kelly's eyes started to tear. I was happy that I'd hurt her. I wanted her to feel at least a little of what I felt.

"I'm sorry, Katie," she pleaded, "I never meant to hurt you."

I didn't respond. After a few minutes she walked away, and I was relieved. I lay back down on my blanket to think.

Eventually the sun was high in the sky, and I knew that a long time had passed. My thoughts finally started to sort themselves out in my head. I needed that. Somehow coming to conclusions about everything helped to calm me down. That was who I was. I liked things organized. I liked knowing what was going to happen next. I liked feeling like I had some sort of control over my own life, and I finally realized that there was nothing wrong with that, it's just who I am.

The first conclusion I came to was that I never, ever wanted to talk to Jake Williams again. I realized that I really didn't know him as well as I thought I had. I used to love him, but I certainly didn't anymore. I guess when someone hurts you that badly, your feelings can change pretty quickly.

I knew that despite some of the things that happened since we started high school, I still had some true friends. Gopi and Gia had really proven that no matter what, they were there for me, and that meant more to me than I could ever explain. I knew that I wanted to be as good of a friend to them, as they'd been to me. I felt bad leaving Jada out of that category, but I also knew it was time to acknowledge that we were drifting apart a little. I hoped it wouldn't continue, but at this point I just wanted to be honest with myself.

I realized that I have an amazing Dad. That he had been everything that my mother wasn't. He worked hard to take care of us, he cooked, he cleaned, he did homework, he  gave rides, he bought dresses, he bought

Christmas gifts, in short he was a good parent, and I was really lucky to have him.

I also realized that my mom was everything he wasn't. She wasn't there for the big events, she wasn't there for my daily life, she had no idea who I was, and I had absolutely no idea who she was.

Worst of all, I finally let myself realize that it had all been her choice. I grabbed the card out of my book bag and looked at it one last time.

*"Happy Birthday! Love, Mom,"* was all it said. She had sent it on our tenth birthday. After seven years away from her kids, all she had to say was, 'Happy Birthday'. I stood up and walked to the edge of the lake, wading in a few inches. The water was freezing and my shoes and socks instantly got wet, but I didn't care. I ran my fingers over the tattered edges of the card one last time, and then I threw it in. As I watched it sink to the bottom, I knew that I

would never stop missing my mom, but I finally saw her for who she really was.

Realizing who my mom was, was what helped me to come to terms with realizing who my sister really was, too. I was right about what I'd said to her earlier, she was just like my mom. She valued herself over other people, including me. My picture perfect version of our relationship was far from the truth, but she was my sister and I couldn't continue hating her forever. At some point we were going to have to start building our relationship back, but I wasn't quite ready for that yet. It was going to take time.

I guess the last, and most important, things that I realized were all about me. In all my thinking and worrying, I had never really thought about who I was before. I always defined myself by who my friends were, by the differences between me and my sister, and by my relationship with Jake. It was time to start figuring out exactly who Katie is, and to learn to be OK with that.

I focused on that for a minute. I know that I'm smart and that I like having things organized and knowing what's going to come next. That's why the last few months had been so hard on me. Change scares me. I admitted to myself just how nervous I get over things, and that I need to learn how to handle it and stop letting it get to me so much. I know that my twin sister is pretty and outgoing and funny, but I made myself admit that I have good qualities too. It's time for me to stop standing in her shadow.

The next one was one of the hardest things for me to think about. I finally admitted to myself that my mom left me when I was three, and she wasn't ever coming back. It was time to try and move on.

Next I admitted that high school was a major change for me, and that maybe I needed to stop trying so hard to make it all OK, and just deal with the fact that it was new and overwhelming until, eventually, it isn't anymore.

Finally, I knew that absolutely nothing was the same as I had thought it was a little less than two months ago when I sat next to this lake and tried to gather my thoughts before my first day at Adam's Prep. The next four years were going to be a roller coaster ride, and absolutely nothing was ever going to be the same.

## About the Author

Andrea Lynch teaches Writing at La Salle University, Camden County College and Paul VI High School. She received her Undergraduate Degree in Communications and Fine Art from Seton Hall University, and a Master's Degree in Writing from Rowan University. Andrea considers all forms of writing, and creative composition and design, her passions.

Andrea enjoys spending time with her two sons, Luke and Jack. They are her inspiration and happiness. Special thanks to them and Ben for their love, patience and support.

***A very special thank you to the students who have inspired me, taught me, made me laugh, reminded me what it's like to be a teenager and made me love teaching.***

## Check out Adam's Prep # 2 - Shades of Kelly

"What's that buzzing?" Alexa, the cheerleading captain, gave me a quizzical look as she held onto my right leg, propping me up for a stunt.

"It's nothing," I tried to blow it off, so they wouldn't know I had snuck my cell into practice. It was completely forbidden to bring your phone to practice because we were supposed to be concentrating solely on cheering.

"No, I hear it too. What is that?" Natalie said, as she held on to my other leg.

I started to panic. I had just been brought up to Varsity this week and now I was gonna blow it.

*Why did I have to bring my phone to practice?* I silently pleaded for my phone to stop and beat myself up for even thinking of hiding it in my pocket.

But the truth was I knew why I'd brought it. It was him. It was always him. He was like a drug, and I was hooked. I couldn't let an hour go by without talking to him. I had almost ruined my whole life because of him, and still for some reason, I just couldn't give him up. Every call, every text, I looked anxiously to see if it said his name. Sometimes it felt like he was all that mattered, and yet, we were still sneaking around.

"That's it for today girls!" Coach Colleen yelled. Relieved I hadn't been found out, I took a deep breath as Nat and Alexa set me down. Instead of learning my lesson and focusing on the sport that I used to live my whole life for, I snuck over to my bag as Colleen talked and sneaked a peek at my phone.

I hit the unlock button and there it was, the new text screen with his name on it. I knew I should ignore it. I knew me and him were toxic together, but I couldn't. I pressed open, closed my eyes, took a deep breath and began wondering just what tonight would bring.

# Want More Info????

# Check Out:
## www.adamsprepbooks.com

# Or E-mail:
## adamsprepbooks@gmail.com

# You can find us on Facebook too!